TRAIN OF GLORY

A FARADAY NOVEL

ROBERT VAUGHAN

WOLFPACK
PUBLISHING
--- EST 2013 ---

Train of Glory

Wolfpack Publishing
6032 Wheat Penny Avenue
Las Vegas, NV 89122

wolfpackpublishing.com

eBook ISBN 978-1-64119-812-7
Paperback ISBN 978-1-64119-813-4

Library of Congress Control Number: 2019934608

AUTHOR'S NOTE

As the Civil War drew to a close, Thomas Nelson Conrad, a Southern intelligence agent, hatched a plan to capture President Abraham Lincoln and hold him for ransom ... not for money, but for concessions to a South that Conrad already knew was defeated. He abandoned his plan, however, when on the day he was to make his move he "beheld the carriage of Mr. Lincoln moving out of the grounds of the White House, preceded and followed by a squad of cavalry."

At about that same time, John Wilkes Booth also came up with the idea of kidnapping Lincoln. But whereas Conrad's plan had the tacit approval of the Confederate government, Booth's did not...nor in fact did the Confederates even know about it. John Wilkes Booth and his small band of coconspirators were acting entirely on their own. When Booth also saw that capturing Lincoln would be too difficult, he made a last-minute change in plans. The whole world knows what followed.

Even with Lincoln's death, the plotting and scheming to capture the President did not cease. In 1876, an attempt was made to steal Lincoln's body and extort money for its return.

The attempt failed, and the body never left the cemetery. Later, when the grave site was renovated, the President's son Robert had the body entombed in a cage of cement and steel rods so it could never again be moved.

While the plot to steal Lincoln's body depicted in this book is fictional, the funeral procession from Washington, D.C., to Lincoln's final resting place in Springfield, Illinois, is recounted with as much historical accuracy as possible. Even the riot in Philadelphia actually took place, and it—like the riot in this story—was caused by pickpockets working the crowd. Three hundred thousand people were involved in the bedlam, which lasted until one in the morning. When order was finally restored, one man was dead from a gunshot wound, the source of which was never determined, and countless people were injured.

Abraham Lincoln's final resting place—along with his wife, Mary Todd, and three of his four sons—is a beautiful spot in Oak Ridge Cemetery, the public cemetery in Springfield, Illinois. One cannot visit there today without seeing in the steady throng of somber visitors the same sense of awe, respect, and sorrow Americans experienced over 120 years ago when millions came out to witness the passing of his funeral train...the Train of Glory.

TRAIN OF GLORY

PROLOGUE

IT WAS DUSK ON APRIL 7, 1865. THE DEEP-PURPLE EVENING sky was streaked with red as the distant Blue Ridge mountains beyond Lynchburg swallowed the setting sun that minutes before had been a glowing fireball. The evening was rapidly growing chilly. At the western edge of a forest outside the small town of Appomattox, a ragtag division of Confederate soldiers was settling down in a comfortless camp. Praying that Union soldiers would not spot the small cooking fires they had just made and batter them with yet another artillery barrage, they wearily prepared their meager supper.

Then in the eerie light, looming like a specter silhouetted against the sky, a horse and faceless rider came galloping toward the edge of the camp.

"Halt! Who goes there?" challenged the nervous sentry, who had been huddling in the trees.

"TAKE IT EASY, son. It's General Barlow," the rider replied, as he slowed his mount and walked him toward the youth. The general swung down from his horse and handed the reins to the sentry.

The general took in the torn, muddied tunic hanging on the spare, youthful frame. Bathed in the blood-red light, the young man's face was lean, his cheeks shadowy with several days' stubble. *My God,* Barlow thought, *he isn't even twenty!* Why he would take note of this young man on this particular evening, Barlow could not say. He had seen hundreds, thousands, like him during this war. He drew a quick breath and said, "Is Colonel Daniels here?"

"Yes, sir," answered the sentry, snapping a salute at the tall, broad-shouldered man. Then, pointing into the trees behind him, the young soldier added, "He's about fifty yards back that-a-way."

As Barlow started into the grove, the young man called after him. "General, sir?"

Barlow stopped and turned around. The dying light of day cast a coppery glow on his handsome face and revealed the deep lines and hollows around his eyes. Earl W. Barlow was only in his mid-thirties, but the horrors he had witnessed during the past four years had marked him indelibly.

The sentry went on, "I hear tell General Lee is gonna give up to the Yankees. Is there any truth to that rumor?"

Barlow let out a long sigh. "I won't lie to you, soldier. I'm afraid he is. Our position here is untenable."

"Yes, sir. Well, I 'spect I'd just as soon have it all over with," the soldier admitted. "If we could get back home early enough, we could still get this year's corn in. The Yankees will let us put in our crops, won't they. General? They ain't got enough room in them Yankee prisons to lock up every last livin' one of us, do they?"

"I'm sure General Lee will secure the best possible peace terms," Barlow assured him.

The sentry shoved his cap askew and scratched his head. "I don't know much about such things as peace terms. I just know one of my brothers was killed at Fredricksburg, another, one at Richmond, and my brother Jamie—well, ain't none of us heard from him since '62, so we don't know where he's at. Sure's gonna be hard, just me and Pa tryin' to put in the crop."

Barlow shook his head. He knew that every man in the Confederate Army was living with the same fears, and he really had no answers to give. But he had been commander for a long time and knew that in these moments of defeat and despair he had to do his best for his men. Thinking quickly, he suggested the first thing that came to mind. "I know all the slaves have been freed, but maybe you can hire a few of the ones who used to work for you."

"Shucks, General, we never did have no slaves. There wasn't nobody workin' that farm but me and my brothers and Pa. That's the way it was with most folks back home." The young soldier laughed bitterly. "I reckon that's funny, ain't it, General? I mean, my brothers and so many other boys gettin' theirselves killed fightin' a war to keep slaves we ain't none of us had."

Barlow looked at the youth curiously. "If you weren't fighting for the right to keep slaves, why were you fighting?"

The lad tossed his head cockily. "Hell, it didn't seem to me like we needed no reason other'n to kick the Yankees in the ass—" Then he dropped his head and mumbled, "'Cept it was us wound up gettin' kicked."

"I expect when it's all over, the Yankees are going to find out we did a little of the kicking, too," Barlow chuckled, hoping to lighten the young man's mood.

The sentry grinned. "Damn right," he declared. "Damn right."

Turning again toward the trees, the general began to pick

his way through the remnants of what had once been a proud division of the Confederate Army. He saw that some of the men were asleep; others were lounging against tree trunks, their rifles lying carelessly on the ground. He passed still other men clustered around the small cook fires and heard the words "surrender" and "get it over with" repeated in muffled tones. The phrases echoed in his ears long after he had moved away from the speakers. Feeling even more morose, Barlow threaded his way deeper into the woods.

He finally spotted Colonel Manley Daniels sitting on a log holding a bottle of whiskey on his knee. The dark-haired man was peering intently into a small fire, his hooded eyes narrowed, his mouth drawn down in a scowl that Barlow knew was habitual. Evidently he had not noticed the general approaching because he did not look up.

Like most of Barlow's men, Daniels had been a farmer before the war began. But Daniels was wealthy, had owned hundreds of slaves, and his plantation was one of the biggest in Georgia. Unlike General Barlow, who was a Virginian, a West Point graduate, and a career army officer, Daniels had had no prior military experience. He had been given his commission as a colonel simply because he had raised and completely equipped his own regiment. Manley Daniels was now, in the closing days of this war, Earl Barlow's second-in-command.

Clearing his throat, Barlow stepped into the circle of fire-light. Daniels glanced up, his expression changing when he recognized his visitor. He did not salute, but he did stand when Barlow approached him. The colonel held out the whiskey bottle, and Barlow accepted, taking a long swig before handing it back.

Before Barlow could thank Daniels for the drink, something heavy smashed through the tree branches about fifty yards away. The muffled sound of an explosion followed seconds later.

"Get down, fellas! Grant's sendin' us some more of his callin' cards!" someone shouted.

Barlow and Daniels dove into a ditch that had been dug earlier that afternoon. A second cannonball burst not more than five feet from where they had been standing, sending iron shards whistling through the tree limbs. Within a few minutes, however, it became clear that the Union gunners had no specific target in mind but were firing their cannons just to harass the Confederate soldiers, and the barrage quickly lifted. As the weary men climbed out of their ditches they heard the distant thunder of artillery being laid down somewhere else.

Daniels and Barlow also climbed out of their ditch. As Daniels brushed himself off, he asked, "What did General Lee think about your plan?"

Barlow's pale blue eyes stared into the distance for a long moment. He took off his hat and ran a weary hand through his blond hair, sighing as he sat down heavily on the log. "I didn't talk to Lee," he replied.

"You didn't even mention the idea?" cried Daniels. "Why not? Did you change your mind?"

"No, I still think my plan is the South's only chance to secure favorable treatment," Barlow remarked.

"Then I don't understand. Why didn't you at least—"

Barlow held up his hand to silence Daniels. "I didn't say anything to him because I was afraid he would say no. I've decided to authorize the action myself."

Daniels's scowl turned into a broad grin, his teeth shining in the pale firelight. "Then we're going to abduct Lincoln and hold him for ransom?"

"Yes," Barlow replied. Then he lowered his voice somewhat. "Colonel, you are well aware of the risks involved. I can't ask you to go with me.

Daniels did not hesitate. "Don't worry about me, General. I want to go."

Barlow nodded. "Then I'll be glad to have you with me. Now, we must get our volunteers together. I know that Dorsey Evans and Buford Posey want to be in on this. They've been with me for the entire war, and I'd like to have them along. You said you had some men who were willing to go."

"Yes, sir, I do," Daniels said eagerly. "I'll go round them up." He started to walk away, moving into the dusky woods out of the dying glow of the small fire.

Suddenly Barlow called, "Oh, and Colonel?"

Daniels stopped and looked back toward him.

"I think you and the others should know that, if we fail, we may well become the most despised figures in human history." As Barlow uttered the words his voice grew bleak. "Judas Iscariot would not be considered so villainous. Have you considered that?"

Colonel Daniels snorted. "What others think doesn't matter."

"Very well." Barlow sighed heavily. "Then we must get started immediately. We're going to have to sneak away tonight and tell no one where we are going or what we are doing. Our own men will think we're deserters."

Daniels shrugged. "Like I said, General. What others think doesn't matter."

"Then God have mercy on us," Barlow muttered. "And I pray that what we're doing is right."

CHAPTER ONE

AS THE TRAIN FROM VIRGINIA CROSSED THE POTOMAC RIVER early on the morning of April 14, Lieutenant Colonel Cole Yeager of the United States Army looked out the window at the city of Washington. A long layer of haze lay over the city, filtering the sun and turning it into a fiery red disk as it rose on the eastern horizon. The smoke from twenty thousand fires—breakfast stoves, fireplaces, and heating furnaces, all lit to push back the chill—formed the haze. With spring not yet a month old, the nights and early mornings were still cold.

Stifling a yawn, Cole stretched his long legs out in front of him. They were stiff and cramped after the long ride from Richmond. He had dozed fitfully during the night and would be glad when the train finally pulled into the depot. The air in the car was close, acrid with smoke from the wood burning in its heating stove and coal oil from the lamps. It was also heavy with the smell of too many people packed too closely together.

As the train clacked into the city, Cole continued to stare out the window. But he did not see the bustling scenes of

Washington beginning a new day. His mind's eye had drifted to one scene that would stay with him for the rest of his life.

Cole was coming to Washington directly from Appomattox, Virginia, where he had witnessed the surrender of Robert E. Lee's forces to General Ulysses S. Grant. He had stood on the steps of the Appomattox courthouse and watched column after column of Confederate soldiers approach the double line of Union soldiers to whom they would formally lay down their arms.

As the battle-thinned regiments of Confederate soldiers neared, marching under their crimson flags, the Union soldiers came to attention. General Gordon, at the head of the Confederate troops, called his men to attention, then saluted the Union soldiers and their officers with his saber. No trumpets blared; no drums rolled. No one uttered a cheer or whispered of victory. An awed stillness reigned over the moment that signaled the end of years of slaughter and a bitter war.

Those vivid images dissolved when the front door of the car opened and the conductor came in...

"Conductor," Cole called, as the official moved down the aisle toward him.

"Yes, sir."

"That building over there," Cole said, pointing through the window. "As I remember, that should be the Capitol, but I don't recognize it."

The conductor chuckled. "I can tell it's been a while since you've been to town, Colonel. That's the Capitol Building, all right—only now it's all decked out with a fancy new dome."

"Very impressive," Cole commented appreciatively.

"Yes, sir, I dare say it is," the conductor agreed. "A man would have to have ice water in his veins not to be stirred by coming to Washington nowadays." He pulled his watch out of his pocket, looked at it, then snapped the case shut. "Five minutes till seven," he announced. "We'll be at the station at exactly seven. Right on time." Smiling briefly at Cole, he continued along the aisle.

True to the conductor's promise, the train pulled into the depot a few moments later, and Cole Yeager disembarked with the other passengers. Pausing briefly on the platform to place his hat on his dark, wavy hair, the officer pulled his uniform cape around him against the chill and scanned the crowded depot to learn where he had to go to collect his bag.

As passersby bustled around him, they cast admiring glances at the towering officer. At six foot four, Cole was the same height as President Abraham Lincoln, but he was not as lean as the country's leader nor as homely. His broad frame was well-muscled, and he had a handsome, rugged face that, at twenty-seven, showed little of the sorrow and horror he had seen in the past five years.

Spotting the baggage claim sign toward the front of the platform, he turned smartly on his heel and threaded his way among the throng. As he worked his way toward it, he mused about how his life would soon change drastically.

Until a few days ago, Cole had been an intelligence officer on General Grant's staff. He had joined Grant at the beginning of the war, fighting alongside him from the early campaigns in Missouri, Kentucky, Tennessee, and Mississippi all the way to the end of the war in Virginia. He had left Appomattox right after the surrender and come to Washington to be discharged from the service and start life as a civilian.

The officer had gone only a few yards when a voice drawled, "Will de colonel be hirin' a hack, or takin' de horsecars?"

Glancing around, Cole saw an old black man wearing a red porter's hat, grinning up at him expectantly. "I'll take the horsecar," he replied.

The man smiled broadly, his twinkling dark eyes approving the choice. "Yes, sir, I figured soon as I laid eyes on you dat you was a practical man and wouldn't be wastin' no money on a hack."

"So that I would be better able to tip you, is that it, my good man?" Cole teased, his blue eyes gleaming. "That one is mine," he added, pointing to a battered bag in a sea of similarly shabby cases that had been unloaded from the baggage car.

"Yes, sir, yes, sir, I 'spect dat's what I had in mind," the black man replied, laughing appreciatively at Cole's good humor. "Course, fightin' in de war like you done, I 'spect you's done enough for folks like me. It sure is happy days around here, now dat de war be over. But then, I reckon you got more reason to be joyful over dat than de rest of us."

"Yes," Cole agreed, "it is a joyful occasion." The wizened porter carried Cole's case to the street and set it down at the horsecar stop. Smiling, Cole tipped him somewhat more generously than was necessary, then turned away from the station to look around. Almost immediately a horsecar drew up. The officer hoisted his bag inside and barely had time to settle in his seat before he was whisked away from the depot. Drawing a deep breath, Cole peered out the window for his first close look at the city he was planning to call home.

What he saw shocked and surprised him. Washington had changed. During the war it had grown into a sprawling city of seventy-five thousand people, but the growth had been sudden and unplanned. What he stared at now was a rather strange jumble of muddy, unpaved streets riddled with potholes and lined with simple, low frame or brick houses. The scene was jarring because these little structures were dominated by a half dozen magnificent marble buildings, built in the classical Greek style, that towered above them.

A canal ran through the middle of the city. Originally

used for small boat traffic, it now was a sluggish, pestilence-breeding waterway that reeked, as John Hay, the President's secretary, often said, "of the ghosts of twenty thousand drowned cats." All the city's sewers emptied into it, and no one could cross the bridges that spanned it without holding his breath against the foul odors.

A half hour later Cole found himself standing in the dimly lit hallway just outside the door of Matthew Faraday's third-floor office on the corner of Tenth and E streets. A sign on the pebbled-glass window of the door read: FARADAY SECURITY SERVICE. The officer took a deep breath, let it out slowly, then knocked on the door.

He had met Matthew Faraday only once five years before in Illinois. Cole had come upon a band of thugs who were ganging up on a silver haired man in a narrow alley near a railroad depot. The man was giving a pretty good accounting of himself, but the odds against him were too great, and the thugs were getting the upper hand. Cole did not know who the man was, who the thugs were, or what the fight was about, but his sense of fair play was outraged. He leapt into the fray on the side of the lone man, and together, they fought the thugs off.

The solitary man was Matthew Faraday, and he offered Cole a job with his security agency on the spot. But Cole turned him down, telling him he was committed to fight in the war.

Once on General Grant's staff serving as an intelligence officer, Cole quickly learned more about Matthew Faraday and his security agency. The distinguished-looking businessman and his network of undercover agents risked their lives on countless dangerous, secret missions for the Union. By the end of the war Cole recognized that Faraday agents had played pivotal roles in keeping the rail lines open. He also knew that Matthew Faraday worked closely with

Secretary of War Stanton and was a friend to President Lincoln.

The door opened, startling Cole. Framed in the doorway was Matthew Faraday himself. The silver haired private detective was somewhere between forty and sixty, a little over six feet tall, and lean with broad shoulders. He stared at Cole for a long moment, his craggy, handsome face perplexed. Suddenly his blue eyes widened.

"Yeager!" he exclaimed, smiling warmly and extending his hand. "Cole Yeager." Then he ran his eyes over the tall young man and took in his Army uniform. "Though I suppose I should say Colonel Yeager."

"Only for one more day, Mr. Faraday," Cole replied. "Tomorrow I'll be a civilian." He smiled with pleasure, adding, "I wasn't sure you'd remember me."

"Of course I remember you! Come inside, please," Faraday stepped back to allow Cole to enter, then closed the door behind him and went on, "You're not an easy man to forget, especially after standing back-to-back with you to fight off that band of ruffians." He laughed heartily. "As I recall, we eventually got the better of them."

"Yes, sir, we did."

Faraday had let Cole into a small room, barely a corridor, that had a door opening beyond it. The businessman gestured toward the inner door and led Cole into a larger room. The morning light flooded into the chamber through a huge window. A scarred old desk piled with papers faced into the room that was clearly an office but nevertheless quite comfortable. Two stuffed chairs stood before the desk, and Faraday motioned to Cole to take one of them as he moved behind the desk. Setting his bag down, Cole sank into the chair.

"Now, before I sit down," Faraday began, "may I get you

some coffee? It's still early, and I was about to have some myself."

Cole nodded and smiled appreciatively, and Faraday slipped from the room. He returned a moment later with a tray that held steaming cups of fragrant coffee and a pitcher of cream and set it down on the cluttered desk.

"Well, to what do I owe the honor? And I do deem your visit an honor," the detective said. He handed a cup to Cole and looked at the young man quizzically.

Cole took a grateful sip from his cup, then said, "Mr. Faraday, you offered me a job back then. I declined, telling you I had a war to take care of first."

"Yes, and you seem to have taken care of it quite well," Faraday said, nodding. Settling into his chair, he watched Cole thoughtfully.

"I must confess, I had a little help," Cole chuckled. "But now that it's over..." He paused and stared into his cup.

"You want to know if the job offer is still open?" Faraday finished the question, his bright blue eyes appraising Cole but revealing nothing. "Yes," Cole answered bluntly.

Faraday's craggy face creased into a wide smile. "It certainly is. How soon do you want to start?"

"Tomorrow, if I may. My release from active duty becomes official at midnight tonight," Cole informed him eagerly. "I'd like to check into a hotel, have a bath and a good meal, and maybe even enjoy a night on the town."

"A night on the town, you say?" Faraday mused, stroking his chin. "Cole, how would you like to start working for me this very evening by doing exactly what you've just said?"

"What do you mean?"

"I have reservations for two in the dining room at Willard's Hotel and tickets for a play tonight at the Ford Theater. They're presenting Our American Cousin. How does that sound?"

"That sounds very good indeed, sir," Cole assured him. "Are you inviting me to go with you?"

Faraday laughed. "No, nothing like that. I'm afraid this is a business assignment. You see, you will be acting as the escort and bodyguard for someone."

"In that case, I'll be glad to start tonight."

"Excellent! You will have to call for the tickets at four. I'm afraid they won't be delivered until later today."

"Then I shall see you at four. By the way, can you suggest a good hotel?"

"Normally I would recommend Willard's, However, I was told that due to the influx of officers returning from the field, Willard's has no vacancies. But you might try the National. It's just a few blocks from here, on Sixth and Pennsylvania." Faraday, gestured to Cole to stand, then motioned him to come around the desk.

Taking him by the elbow, Faraday stepped over to his window and pointed. "Oh, and do you see that building right across the street? That's Ford's Theater."

Cole Yeager looked across at Ford's Theater. Plastered across the front of the building was a large sign that read:

BENEFIT
—AND—
LAST NIGHT
OF
MISS LAURA KEENE
SUPPORTED BY MR. JOHN DYOTT AND MR. HARRY
HAWK IN
OUR AMERICAN COUSIN

Turning from the window, Cole said, "Well, that certainly makes things convenient, doesn't it? I guess I'll head over to the hotel right now and get myself a room—assuming there's one available, of course."

With a smile he turned and retrieved his bag, and Faraday walked him to the outer door. "If you have any difficulty, let me know. Otherwise, I'll plan on seeing you back here later this afternoon."

The National Hotel was a massive, red-brick building, so large that it occupied an entire block between Pennsylvania and C streets on Sixth Avenue. Cole could hot help gawking at the impressive structure as he approached it. A fine marquee, swathed in red, white, and blue bunting, covered the entrance, and Old Glory fluttered proudly above it. Even the doorman sported a red, white, and blue rosette in his lapel.

The ostentatious display of patriotism might have been in celebration of the end of the war— or it might have been put on because, as some of the more cynical Washingtonians were saying, the National was trying to live down its prewar reputation as the hotel of choice for Southern senators and congressmen.

As Cole stepped under the marquee and started toward the grand entrance, he smiled at the doorman who hurriedly opened the door for him. Stepping into the spacious lobby, Cole paused and scanned the well-appointed, crowded room, then crossed to the front desk and inquired about a room.

"Yes, Colonel, we do have rooms available," the smiling desk clerk answered. "We are always proud to host our brave lads who are returning to us after the war. Just sign here, please." As Cole, signed the register, the clerk read the inscription, and his eyes widened with interest. "Lieutenant Colonel Cole Yeager, Headquarters Staff, General Grant. So, you know the General, do you?"

"Yes," Cole replied noncommittally.

"The General, I understand, is staying at Willard's Hotel. If you could convince him to move to the National, we would be so grateful that your lodging would be free for as long as you stayed with us."

Cole chuckled. "Mister, I haven't managed to persuade General Grant to change his mind on anything for the last five years."

"Yes, well, it was just a thought." The clerk sighed, clearly disappointed.

At that moment, a strikingly handsome young man dressed in riding clothes strode through the lobby. The clerk spotted him, straightened, and nudged Cole excitedly. "Do you see that man?" he whispered, as he pointed to him. "That's John Wilkes Booth, a very famous actor. He's one of our guests," he added proudly. "Would you like to meet him?"

Before Cole could answer, the clerk called to Booth. The dark-haired man smiled and headed toward the counter.

Cole appraised him as he worked his way through the crowd. He knew that Booth's brother, Edwin, was actually more famous; nevertheless, there was something magnetic about this intense, dark-eyed man.

"Mr. Booth!" the clerk exclaimed, evidently relishing the opportunity to introduce the actor. "This is Cole Yeager, a lieutenant colonel on General Grant's staff."

"I was on his staff," Cole gently corrected the clerk. "As of midnight tonight, I will no longer be in the army."

"Nevertheless, he is one of the real heroes of this war," the clerk went on.

"I wouldn't say hero," Cole replied, growing increasingly uncomfortable with the clerk's need to embellish what little he knew.

Booth eyed Cole and brushed his thick dark mustache with a gloved finger. "Yes, actually, to call a Union colonel a hero or villain would depend on which side one's sympathies lay, wouldn't it?" he finally observed wryly.

Cole thought it was a rather strange thing to say, but Booth then tempered the remark with a broad smile.

"Perhaps I shall get to see some of your heroics tonight," Cole suggested. "I'll be attending *Our American Cousin*."

"Oh, then you won't see Mr. Booth," the clerk put in quickly. "He isn't in that play."

Booth smiled oddly, a mysterious, peculiar expression. Then, holding up a finger and waving it dramatically, he declared, "Nevertheless, eColonel, I do believe you'll see a particularly fine performance tonight." He touched the brim of his riding cap and continued on his way.

Cole watched him go, then sighed as if to dismiss the queer encounter and turned back to the clerk. "I trust you have facilities for a bath?" he asked.

"You will be on the fifth floor, Colonel. Though your room isn't equipped with a private bathing room, there is a public bath located at the end of the hall. It has a stove for heating your water."

"That will do nicely." Taking the key from the clerk, Cole picked up his bag and began climbing the broad, carpeted stairway to his floor.

As he ascended, he began to wonder what he would wear that evening. For the past four years he had not had to consider that. Whenever he had a formal occasion to attend —and since he served on Grant's staff, there were several— he wore his uniform, and it was as acceptable as formal evening attire. Yet in a matter of hours he would be a civilian again and would have to start thinking a little differently. Perhaps it was time to begin making some changes.

During the closing days of the war, an enterprising tailor had visited the troops, taking orders from the men who would be returning to civilian life and would need new clothes. Cole had ordered a suit from the bustling little man, and now he was glad. He would wear his suit, he decided, even though it would feel strange. When he reached his room, he took the suit out of his bag and hung it up, hoping it would be wrinkle-free by dinnertime.

In a less prosperous part of the city, in the Dunn Hotel—a smaller, seedier establishment than either the National or the Willard—Brigadier General Earl W. Barlow and his second in command, Colonel Manley Daniels, were meeting with their men. They had all managed to slip away from Appomattox just before the surrender, had traveled to Washington separately, and were meeting as a group for the first time in Barlow's shabby, first floor room.

The tense meeting had been under way for half an hour, and cigar smoke hung in a heavy haze in the small room. Barlow, who was standing with his back to the window, turned and pushed it open to let the gray-blue cloud escape into the gloomy, litter-filled alleyway. He swung around and faced the five volunteers.

The cigar-smoker clouding the air in the small room was Sergeant Dorsey Evans. Loyal to Barlow since an episode at the beginning of the war had bound them together, Evans—a dark-haired, slightly built man in his thirties—was the man Barlow knew he could count on most in this group.

Evans had recruited a fellow Tennessean, Buford Posey, a full-faced private in his early twenties with wide blue eyes. The shy private rarely spoke, preferring to let Evans talk and then nod his dusty blond head vigorously in agreement. Posey would follow Evans anywhere.

The three men Daniels had brought to the band were a different sort entirely. All former privates and Georgians, Pete Chambers, Lee Hawkins, and Alan Tatterwall were part of the regiment Daniels had personally raised and equipped. Because the three were always together and vaguely resembled each other, Barlow could not readily tell them apart. They were all in their late twenties, of medium build, with light brown hair. Pete Chambers had dusty blue eyes, while the other two had murky brown eyes. During the war the trio sometimes went on long, secretive scouting missions and always returned with booty—captured weapons, horses, food—that Barlow knew they had stolen.

Barlow glanced at Daniels, standing beside him, and went on, "Now, are there any questions so far?"

"Yes, sir, I got one, General," Dorsey Evans said around his stogie.

"Please, Sergeant Evans—that is, Dorsey—feel free to speak."

"Thank you, General. Well, sir, now that the war is over, who's goin' to be doin' the talkin' for us, once we complete our mission? I mean, technically there's no such thing as a Confederate government anymore, is there?"

"That's a good question, Dorsey," Barlow replied, running his hand thoughtfully through his thick blond hair. "To answer you honestly, there is no authorized body in charge. But, then, there never was a legal Confederate government or even an army. As you know, I was a career army officer before the war started. I gave up my commission to fight for the Confederacy because I am a Virginian and I believe in this cause, I was made a general, but—and this is important— I held that rank only because you and the other men dedicated to the same cause accepted me as such. Therefore, if we accept that what we are doing is right, then our authority is justified."

"I'll tell you where our authority lies," Manley Daniels declared, "It lies in success. If we're able to take Lincoln prisoner and hold him hostage until the Yankees agree to our terms, that is all the authority we need."

"Colonel Daniels is quite correct, of course," Barlow

went on, giving Daniels an approving nod. "We must succeed. Our very survival depends upon it. I think you all understood the risks when you volunteered for this mission last week." Then Barlow's handsome face grew somber. "Since then, however, General Lee has surrendered. Only Johnston is still in the field, and I feel his capitulation is imminent. If any of you want to change your minds, I will understand."

"General, whatever it takes, you can count on us," Dorsey said fervently. "And I think I'm speakin' for all of us. Would you agree, Buford?"

Buford Posey's broad face was wreathed in a smile. "That's right, General. As far as I'm concerned, the war ain't over 'til you say it's over." Tatterwall, Chambers, and Hawkins glanced quickly at Daniels, then nodded.

Barlow smiled in relief. "I knew I could count on you men," he told them.

Suddenly Daniels reached into his pocket, took out a piece of paper, and handed it to Barlow. "General, I picked up this handbill today. They're all over town. It says that Lincoln and Grant will be attending a play tonight at Ford's Theater."

Barlow scanned it, then looked up at Daniels questioningly.

"Maybe this is the chance we've been looking for," Daniels suggested eagerly. "Maybe we can capture Lincoln tonight at the play."

The general shook his head. "No, there will be too many people around. Someone is sure to come to the President's assistance, and if they do, they might get hurt."

"We're at war, General," Daniels observed, his dark eyes narrowing angrily. "People get hurt in war."

"Yes," Barlow agreed evenly, "but I want to remind you that we're trying to win favorable concessions for the South.

And it won't help our cause if we injure—or perhaps even kill innocent people."

"Yes, General, but I want to remind you that there are Yankees who plan to strip the South of all it has," Daniels remarked, his voice tight. "We must move, and we must move quickly if, by abducting Lincoln, we intend to have any effect on their evil designs."

Barlow studied Manley Daniels's scowling face. "Would you have us move thoughtlessly, Colonel, or would you have us move by plan?"

Daniels stiffened, his hooded eyes staring at the thread-bare carpet. "By plan," he conceded.

Barlow folded his arms across his broad chest. "Good. I'm glad to hear that."

"What is your plan, General?" Dorsey Evans asked.

The general glanced at the sergeant's lean, trusting face. "I think perhaps the best idea would be for Colonel Daniels and me to attend this play tonight. That will give us the opportunity to see just how the President is guarded. And, more importantly, how well he obeys the instructions his guards give him."

"They say when he came to be inaugurated the first time, he sneaked into Washington dressed like a woman," Daniels scoffed. "That should speak for the coward he is."

Barlow shook his head. "That simply isn't true; I was still in the Federal Army at that time and was in Washington when Lincoln arrived. He appeared without notifying anyone, yes, because rumors of his assassination were rampant. However, he was not disguised as a woman and, whatever you may have heard, I assure you that Abraham Lincoln is no toward."

"You sound almost as if you admire the man," Daniels snapped accusingly.

"I suppose it does sound strange," Barlow admitted,

"because I hold Abraham Lincoln personally responsible for the defeat of the South and the end of all I hold dear. But logically, if he's responsible for that, I must also give him credit for uniting the North and leading it to victory. All this from a man most people used to regard as a buffoon."

"Buffoon? Baboon is a better word," Daniels sneered, and everyone but Barlow laughed.

The general shook his head slowly. "Don't underestimate the man," he warned. "To do that would be to repeat the same mistake the Confederate government made." He suddenly smiled. "And I assure you, gentlemen, I do not plan on making any mistakes."

In the public bathing room at the end of the fifth-floor hall in the National Hotel, Tamara Goodnight had just finished her bath. As she stood up, she removed the hairpin that was holding her thick, red-gold hair in a coil on the top of her head and let it fall loosely about her pale shoulders. Then she reached for the towel she had left on a nearby chair. Finding it beyond her grasp, she stepped out of the tub. The pretty, rosy-cheeked young woman began humming a time as she moved toward the chair. Suddenly the door to the hall was thrown open, and the song died in her throat.

Tamara gasped as she found herself staring at a very tall, muscular man dressed in the uniform of an army officer. He had a towel draped across one arm, while his other hand clutched a shaving mug, brush, and razor. He looked as shocked to see Tamara as she did to see him. However, his look of surprise quickly turned to one of interest as he stood admiring her beauty.

"Well, good morning, ma'am," he said as easily as if he were passing her on the street.

Tamara had been so shocked by his sudden appearance that for a long moment she did not attempt to cover herself. Only when she saw his appreciative expression did she come to her senses. Quickly she grabbed the towel and threw it around herself, managing to restore some modesty, if not dignity. "Who are you, sir? And why are you here?" she demanded.

"I am Colonel Cole Yeager." He held up his towel and smiled. "And I am here to take a bath."

"Yes, well, as you can clearly see, this bathing room is occupied," Tamara said hurriedly.

"Yes, ma'am, I can plainly see that."

Her amber eyes narrowing, Tamara countered, "You are an officer, sir—and that presupposes you are also a gentleman. I've never known a gentleman to barge into a lady's bath."

"I'm sorry, ma'am," he replied sincerely. He gestured at the door, then added, "I was told only that the bathing room was at the end of the hall. I had no way of knowing anyone was in here. I heard no sound, and the door was unlocked."

"I...I thought I did lock the door," Tamara murmured, disconcerted as she realized that the situation was partly her fault.

Cole Yeager touched his right eyebrow in a salute. "Finish your bath in peace, ma'am. I shall stand guard outside your door." With that, he withdrew and pulled the door shut behind him.

Quickly Tamara dried herself. She was appalled by the incident, and she blushed furiously as she dressed. She admitted to herself that part of her embarrassment stemmed from the fact that she found her intruder terribly handsome —and that she should meet such a man under these conditions was mortifying.

Once her dressing was completed, she opened the door, hoping to find the officer gone. Instead, he was standing in the hall, faithfully discharging his promise to protect her from any further intrusion.

"I see you are still here," she commented, trying to make her voice sound flat and unemotional.

"Yes, and lucky for you," he told her. "There was another man who would have walked in on your bath had I not turned him away."

"I thank you, Colonel," Tamara responded coolly.

He looked at her face intently, his blue eyes suddenly serious, "Please forgive me. I sincerely hope you do not think I planned my ill-timed entry. I'm afraid I've been in the field for too long, and I didn't use any common sense. I was so anxious to bathe in a real bathtub instead of an icy stream that I didn't stop to think that someone else might be inside. I most heartily apologize, and I wouldn't blame your husband if he called me out."

Mollified by his obvious discomfort, Tamara smiled. "I am not married, Colonel. And I confess it's partly my fault for not making certain that the door was locked. But please, let's not speak of it anymore. I find this most embarrassing."

He smiled in return. "I have already forgotten," he told her, stepping into the bathroom. "Uh, Miss?" he suddenly called.

Tamara, eager to put the awkward situation behind her, had already started down the hall. Stopping, she turned and looked at him. "Yes?"

"I realize this is terribly impertinent of me, but I was wondering if you might have dinner with me tonight? You see, I just..." He stopped in midsentence, then shook his head and sighed. "I'm sorry. I just remembered I already have an engagement tonight."

"It's just as well. I'm also engaged this evening," she replied. Then she smiled archly. "And besides, now that the war is over, I think such impromptu socializing between men and women will once again become improper, don't you?"

"I suppose so," he admitted, his face glum.

"Good day, Colonel. I hope you have a pleasant bath."

Continuing to her room, Tamara went inside and closed the door behind her. She then crossed to the window and looked out over the city, trying to compose herself. Her face was flushed, she knew, and she felt a shortness of breath— and she was not sure it was all because of the embarrassing incident. Tamara was glad that the colonel had another engagement tonight... and she was glad she did as well. Otherwise she might have been tempted to accept his invitation, as bold as it may have been.

And what if I had? Tamara wondered. She was certainly no longer a child, not at twenty-six, and during the past four years she had seen and experienced things that no one should have to endure. She had earned the right to live her own life without regard to what others might think— and she had earned the right to have a little enjoyment, just as that colonel had.

Colonel Cole Yeager was no Washington drawing-room officer. He was a man who had seen battle and had looked death in the face. Tamara knew this because she had seen it in his eyes. Even when he smiled, there was a screen—far in the back of his eyes—that hid the pain and horror from sight. The screen was effective when the colonel was dealing with most people, but Tamara was not most people. She was expert in seeing it—and in seeing through it. During the war, she had held men's hands as they died, being mother, sister, wife, and sweetheart to them as they called out in their delirium. She had written last letters home for them and had read letters from home to them. She had bathed their wounds, applied their bandages, and wrapped their severed arms and legs in blankets to be carried away.

Yes, Colonel Yeager and she had earned the right to have

a pleasant meal together, to talk about things other than suffering and death, to eat good food and drink fine wine.

Tamara strode across the room and put her hand on the doorknob. For one brief moment she thought of walking back down the hall, barging in on his bath as he had on hers, and telling him not to do whatever it was he was supposed to do that night while she broke her own engagement. Then as quickly as the notion had come up it went away, and Tamara felt herself blushing again, this time for allowing the fantasy to go so far unchecked. Telling herself that she really must learn to think more modestly, she returned to the window and began studying the city.

CHAPTER TWO

At four o'clock that afternoon a different-looking Cole Yeager appeared at the Faraday Security Service office. The uniform was gone, replaced by a dark suit, starched white shirt, silk vest, and cravat.

Matthew Faraday led the young man into his office and, when they were both seated, commented on the change. The detective, who was an astute judge of men, had instantly sensed Cole's discomfort and decided to put him at ease.

"I hope this suit is acceptable," Cole said as he tugged a little nervously at his starched collar. "I've been away from civilian life for so long that I no longer have any idea how to dress properly."

Faraday laughed warmly. "Cole Yeager, I suspect that whatever you wore, it would be appropriate," he assured him. "I think you look fine and I think you'll make an excellent escort for the lady tonight."

"The lady?" Cole asked, surprised.

"Yes. Didn't I tell you whom you were escorting?"

Shaking his head, Cole replied, "No, you said only that I would be both escort and bodyguard."

"Oh, I'm sorry I didn't give you more information. You are, of course, familiar with the work of the Sanitary Commission?"

"Certainly," Cole said. "The Sanitary Commission provided all kinds of services for the military during the war. They opened canteens and served food at the railroad depots in all the major cities, assisted traveling soldiers and sailors, and gave medical aid on the battlefield. As I recall, the organization took its name from a British agency established by Florence Nightingale during the Crimean War." He paused, a faraway look in his blue eyes, then concluded, "Yes, their service was indispensable."

Faraday nodded. "I remember that when they started they faced quite an uphill struggle. President Lincoln wasn't convinced such an organization was necessary. I believe he called it 'a fifth wheel on a coach.' But he soon changed his mind and became one of the Sanitary Commission's biggest supporters. In fact, President Lincoln insisted on inviting one of the Commission's nurses to Washington to participate in the celebration ceremonies. She is representing all the 'Angels of the Battlefield,' and she's the lady you'll be escorting to dinner and the theater this evening."

"Mr. Faraday, this is an honor," Cole declared, smiling. Then his voice softened as he went on, "I often saw the beneficial effect those gentle ladies had. More than once I was the recipient myself...although I was never seriously injured."

Faraday looked at him thoughtfully. "Yes," he said gently. "You know, I recall that the nurses had a difficult time of it at first. Many people argued that it was all right for women to serve food at the rail depots, but they had no place in field hospitals. It was said that they would be exposed to intimate, sordid details that no respectable woman should see."

Cole was nodding, his blue eyes peering over Faraday's shoulder at a distant memory. "Well, they certainly were often in the thick of things," he mumbled. "Sometimes they had to scurry along with the rest of us to the bombproofs to avoid the artillery barrages. But the nurses proved their value many times over. I recall a particular gray-haired old woman who was a mother to us all at Fredericksburg." Cole smiled and turned his gaze back to Faraday. "No matter which nurse was chosen to be their symbol, I will escort her proudly tonight. It's the least I can do to repay those dedicated ladies for all they did for us."

Grinning a little mysteriously, Faraday picked up an envelope from the pile of papers on his desk and handed it to Cole. "Here is the lady's name and where you are to meet her. And here, too, are your tickets." Then smiling benevolently, he went on, "The waiter will not even deliver a check to your table. Your dinner is already taken care of."

Cole glanced at the envelope, then looked up at Faraday. "I see I am to meet her in the lobby of the National Hotel," he observed. "That's convenient."

"Yes, isn't it?" Faraday agreed. Still smiling, he rose, moved around the desk, and escorted Cole to the door. "Let me know how it goes, won't you?" he asked.

"Of course," Cole agreed, returning the smile. "After all, this is my very first assignment as a Faraday agent."

At ten minutes to six, Cole Yeager stepped into the lavishly decorated lobby of the National Hotel. The gas chandeliers glittering overhead bathed the room in a soft yellow glow. An ornate parlor stove had already been lit to warm the high-ceilinged room against the evening's chill, and it smelled of smoke, mingled with the perfumes of elegantly dressed women who strolled by him on the arms of their escorts on their way to dinner.

Spotting the uniformed majordomo, he approached the man and informed him that he was waiting to meet someone. Should a lady inquire about him, he told him, he would appreciate it if the man would point him out. Then tipping the smiling man, he strolled to one of the crimson- covered armchairs and settled down.

Realizing that he was early and noticing a copy of the *Washington Evening Star* lying on the polished table next to him, he picked up the paper and scanned the first page. He was so engrossed in his reading that he did not notice when someone, approached him five minutes later and was startled by a discreet cough. Quickly he closed the paper and glanced up.

Standing before his chair was the woman he had intruded upon earlier. She was dressed in a forest-green velvet gown with a low-cut neckline and carried a matching silk shawl. Her hair was pulled back stylishly from her face and tumbled in ringlets about her pale shoulders.

"Good evening, Colonel Yeager," she said, her amber eyes twinkling in a wry smile.

Cole stood quickly, delighted that she had come over to speak to him. "Hello," he replied. "It's good to see you again. I mean..." He stopped, embarrassed, then cleared his throat.

She laughed heartily. "I know what you mean," she told him. "And please don't apologize anymore."

"I'm sorry. I won't apologize anymore."

She smiled up at him playfully. "So you're apologizing for apologizing."

Cole grinned sheepishly. "I guess I am," he admitted. "I'm sorry." Then they both laughed.

"Colonel, I've thought about your invitation this evening. Perhaps over the dinner table we can become friends, and the awkward scene this afternoon can be forgotten. Are you ready to go?"

"Go?" Cole asked in confusion.

"Yes, to dinner."

"Oh." He was keenly disappointed and then felt his face

flush. "Oh, I'm sorry. Don't you remember? I told you, I have another engagement this evening. I am to escort some elderly nurse to dinner and the theater."

"An elderly nurse?"

"Yes. Believe me, I can think of no greater pleasure than to take you to dinner, but—"

"But you have an odious task to perform. Am I correct?" she asked, finishing his sentence for him.

Cole shook his head. "No. No, I didn't say that. I said nothing would give me greater pleasure than to take you to dinner. But you see I do have this commitment. Even though I've never met this lady, I did meet many of her sisters during the war, and I consider escorting her tonight to be a great privilege."

Tamara's eyes twinkled, and she tossed her head lightly. "I'm very glad to hear you say that. You see, Colonel, it is my turn to apologize. I have been having a little fun with you! I am Tamara Goodnight—the nurse you are to escort."

Cole's blue eyes widened in surprise. "You? But I thought...that is, I was led to believe—"

"That you would be escorting a motherly old lady," Tamara repeated, laughing. "Yes, I know. Mr. Faraday told me whom you were expecting. I think he decided to surprise you by not shattering your illusions. I hope you aren't too disappointed."

Cole shook his head vigorously, and a delighted grin spread across his face. "Disappointed? Miss Goodnight, this could well be the most pleasant duty I've ever performed."

"Then, shall we go?" Tamara asked, placing her gloved hand on Cole's forearm and smiling up at him warmly.

The elegant dining room at Willard's Hotel was festively yet tastefully decorated. Nestled in crystal vases in the center of each white-damask-covered table were red roses tied with blue ribbons. A rich maroon brocade covered the walls, and a soft rosy glow cast by the discreetly placed chandeliers and winking candles suffused the room.

Tamara and Cole had been led to a corner table that was shielded from the other diners by some potted palms. There they feasted on a perfectly prepared meal of baby lamb chops, spring peas, boiled potatoes, fresh garden salad, and bread still warm from the oven. The waiter had just set a fragrant slice of hot pecan pie topped with a dollop of cream in front of each of them and was pouring steaming coffee into the fine china cups. It was a meal to remember—unlike any either of them had had in quite some time.

"Have you enjoyed your dinner?" Cole asked as he smiled at her across the table.

Tamara's amber eyes glistened happily in the candle light. "With considerably more relish than the meals I had at Cedar Creek," she replied warmly.

"You were at Cedar Creek?" he asked in surprise.

"Yes," she replied, putting down her fork. "Our field hospital was set up in the Episcopal Church at Middletown."

Cole stared over her shoulder, seeing the past. "I remember that hospital very well," he mused. Then he pulled himself back to the present and looked into her eyes. "You see, though I didn't find out about it until later, a good friend of mine died there. His name was Major Mike Morris."

"I knew your friend," Tamara said softly. "They called him 'Iron Mike.' We tried desperately to save him, but his wounds were too serious." Pausing, she pushed her cup away and lowered her eyes. "I can understand why he was your friend. I haven't met a more gracious man, and his courage and spirit never wavered even though he was in terrible pain. I held his hand until the end...There was nothing else I could do for him...and, just before he died, he thanked me."

Then she looked up at him and pressed her lips together. Tears welled in her eyes. Cole reached across the table and took her hand in his. "Tamara," he began, his voice hoarse with emotion, "let's make tonight a celebration of life. Let's enjoy it not only for ourselves, but for Mike and for everyone like him who can't be here."

"I think that's a wonderful idea," she agreed, smiling through her tears.

Lifting his wine glass, Cole proposed, "To life— and all that it has to offer." Tamara raised her glass and tapped it gently against his, and then they both drank deeply.

When they finished their meal. Cole realized there was plenty of time to spare before the play began. Outside the restaurant, the couple found several carriages-for-hire parked in front of the hotel. Cole summoned one of them, suggesting a drive around the city. Tamara readily agreed and climbed into the landau, settling into the seat and wrapping her shawl tightly around her shoulders.

Both of them had been to Washington before the war and commented now on how much the city had changed. When they passed the White House, lit brightly by gas lamps, Cole remarked, "I can imagine that no one is happier the war is over than the man who lives there."

"Have you ever met him?" Tamara asked.

"No, but I know his son Robert. He joined General Grant's staff toward the end of the war and was with us at Appomattox. Have you met the President?"

"Not yet," Tamara replied. "But I am to sit in the reviewing stand with the President's party during the grand parade celebrating the end of the war." She shivered with excitement. "My friends and family back home will be quite thrilled to hear of that," she added.

"Where is your home?"

"Boston. And yours?"

"Galena, Illinois," Cole replied. Tamara shivered again, and he asked solicitously, "Cold?"

"Yes, a little," she admitted, leaning against him for warmth. "I should have brought a warmer wrap."

He put his arm around her and murmured, "How glad I am that you didn't." They sat looking silently at each other for a long moment, then Cole called up front, "Driver, perhaps we should go to the theater now."

"Yes, sir," the driver answered, and he turned the team in the proper direction. A few minutes later the landau stopped in front of Ford's Theater.

As Cole helped Tamara out of the carriage he noticed the large, excited crowd of elegantly dressed people milling under the theater's marquee. He heard the words "the President" mentioned many times, as well as frequent references to General Grant.

"If the people here are expecting to see General Grant, I'm afraid they're going to be disappointed," Cole whispered to Tamara. "I know that the General and his wife are leaving the city tonight in order to be with their children."

"But the President will be here, won't he?" Tamara asked.

"I don't know. They say he will," he answered, gesturing to the crowd.

"I should like to see him at least once before I join his party on the reviewing stand," she whispered, her face aglow with awe and delight.

Inside the lobby they noticed that the crowd was thinning somewhat as the theater patrons began to move to their seats. The tickets Matthew Faraday had given Cole were for seats in the dress circle. As they started up the stairs they met a very handsome young man who was coming down.

He smiled and said, "Well, Colonel, I see that you did come tonight. I hope you enjoy the performance."

"Thank you, I shall," Cole answered.

The man continued down the stairs and melted into the crowd in the lobby.

Tamara watched him go and then turned to her companion. "Cole, wasn't that John Wilkes Booth, the actor?" she asked.

"Yes," he replied, looking down at her warily.

"My goodness, I didn't know you knew him. You should have introduced us!" she exclaimed, her eyes wide with curiosity.

Cole grinned sheepishly. "I only met him today," he admitted. "And while my years fighting in the war may have caused my manners to grow rusty, they did not cause me to take leave of my common sense. I would not want to introduce such a handsome man to a beautiful woman—especially if I am privileged by chance to be that woman's escort."

Tamara smiled up at him and playfully squeezed his arm. "Cole Yeager, you should know that not every woman is attracted to such a drawing-room dandy. I'm quite pleased with my escort of the evening; thank you."

In Taltval's Star saloon, which was located just to the right of the theater, Earl Barlow and Manley Daniels were sitting at a small table in the back of the dimly lit, smoke-filled room having a drink. The saloon was crowded that evening; many of its patrons had come to catch a glimpse of the President as he entered the theater next door.

"Maybe he won't even be here," Daniels suggested in a hoarse whisper. "Grant isn't."

"A last-minute change of plans, I understand," Barlow replied with a shrug. "But I'm sure Lincoln will attend the play. I overheard one of the theater's employees say that even though Grant won't be here, the President will."

"Then that's perfect!" Daniels exclaimed. "I didn't know if my plan could work with Grant in the box, but without him, I feel certain we can abduct the President tonight."

"Impossible," Barlow snapped. "You know we've only

come here tonight to observe how closely the President is guarded."

"I know, but I've thought this out, and I think it will work. Won't you at least hear my plan?"

Daniels's voice was so plaintive that the general regretted his hasty reply. "All right, Colonel, I'll listen to your plan," Barlow agreed. "I don't ever want it said that I didn't at least examine every opportunity."

Pushing his drink aside, Daniels leaned forward and clasped his hands on the table in front of him. "This is how it would work," he began. "We'll position one of our men by the main gas valve. By a simple twist of the wrist, he can plunge the entire theater into darkness. Of course, it must all be precisely timed, because the instant the theater is dark we must strike. You and I will be waiting just outside the President's box where we will overpower his guards and him. We'll bind and gag him, then lower him over the railing where two of our men will be waiting on the stage. Meanwhile, two more will be waiting with a covered carriage in the alleyway behind the theater. We will vault from the box to the stage, make our way into the alley, then leave. A few of our men, armed with pistols, will linger in the alley to hold off any pursuers, and afterward, they can ride very hard to catch up with us."

Barlow was silent and drummed his fingers on the table for a long moment. *Daniels has always been so impulsive,* he thought. *This is much too complicated.*

Daniels, his patience wearing thin, began to fidget and finally asked, "Well, what do you think of the plan?"

"Manley, it's a bold plan, and if we were desperate to make the abduction tonight, it would be one with some merit. But we don't need to be so hasty. Why rush into a plan of such desperation?"

Daniels's jaw tightened, and he was clearly angry. "The plan would work, General," he insisted, his voice rising.

Barlow shook his head in warning and gestured to him to drop his voice. "Don't you realize that the instant the lights went out everyone in the theater would rush to the presidential box? That the entire audience would fear some sort of foul play?"

"That's why we would have to depend upon precise timing," the colonel argued in a harsh whisper.

"And even if we were successful to the point that we actually got him outside, someone would be sure to follow. That would mean shooting, and innocent people might get hurt...maybe killed."

"General, no matter what our plan, there's going to be some risk," Daniels reminded him.

"I agree. But I owe it to our men to reduce the risk to the absolute minimum. If I agree to try your idea, I would want to have a few rehearsals. You have even admitted that the plan would require very precise timing, and that would take practice."

Sighing heavily, Daniels acquiesced. "All right, General, if you say so."

Barlow smiled and, leaning across the table, put his hand on the colonel's shoulder. "Don't be glum, my friend. It was a good plan. It's just too bad you didn't come up with it earlier so we would have the opportunity to put it into operation." He sat back in his chair and added, "Don't worry. We'll accomplish our mission. We'll take a real good look at the kind of protection the President has, and we'll come up with a way to do it."

Brightening, Daniels remarked, "In that case, I guess we'd best finish our drinks and get to the theater. We want to be seated by the time the President arrives."

Across the street from the bar, on the third floor of the

corner office building, Matthew Faraday was just leaving his office. He was locking the outer door when he heard foot-steps coming up the stairs. Turning toward the sound, he made out the shadowy form of William Crook, the personal bodyguard to Abraham Lincoln. Matthew Faraday had secured that job for him.

"Matthew?" Crook called out as he reached the head of the stairs and peered into the dimly lit hallway.

"Yes, Bill. What can I do for you?"

"Ah, I thought that was you," Crook replied. He yawned, then apologized. "Excuse me, but I've been on duty since five-thirty this morning."

"And you're just now getting off?" asked Faraday, appalled at the idea. Acting as bodyguard to the President was an exhausting, demanding job.

Crook rubbed his cheek wearily. "Yes. I was supposed to be relieved at four, but my replacement didn't arrive until after seven."

"I would say your relief isn't a very dependable man," Faraday said, working to keep his anger in check.

Crook sighed disgustedly. "You can say that again," he replied. "It's John Parker."

"Parker? He is the President's bodyguard tonight? Hasn't he been reprimanded for drunkenness on duty a few times?"

"Among other things," Crook said, shaking his head. Then he drew himself up and looked squarely at Faraday. "Which brings me to why I'm here. Matthew, I wonder if you would consider going to the play tonight...as the President's guest."

Faraday was surprised. "Has the President invited me?"

Crook quickly averted his eyes. "Well, no," he admitted.

Smiling, the agent said, "Bill, I would be delighted to go, but I have a very pressing engagement tonight. I would break it...if the President had invited me. But I'm afraid it would be highly improper of me to invite myself."

Crook looked back at Faraday; this time worry and sorrow were etching lines around his eyes. "It's just that I'm concerned about tonight," he confessed. "I don't trust Parker."

Searching the man's face, Faraday asked softly, "You don't believe Parker means the President any harm, do you?"

"No, I don't mean that. But I don't trust him to be vigilant tonight...of all nights."

"Why are you so concerned about tonight?" Faraday asked, a puzzled frown on his craggy face. "I would think, now that the war is over, the danger to the President would be less."

"Perhaps it is," Crook conceded, "but it's—Damn it, Matthew, it's just that I have an uneasy feeling tonight. I guess it's crazy."

Faraday shook his head. "No, Bill," he said flatly. "I've been in this business too long not to pay attention to such feelings. Tell me a little more. What happened today? Have you seen or heard anything that causes you to feel this way?"

"Not really. It's just that..." Crook broke off, then began again. "Tonight, when I left the White House, the President said, 'Good-bye, Crook.' Good-bye, not good night. He's never said anything but good night before. If I weren't so tired, I'd go myself."

Rubbing his chin thoughtfully, Faraday was silent for a moment. "All right," he promised gently. "I'll have to go across town to make my apologies—I can't very well leave my friends wondering what happened to me. I'm afraid it'll be too late to join the President's party before he leaves the White House, but I'll get to the theater as soon as I can." He pulled out his watch. "I don't see how I can get over there and back before ten o'clock, though."

"That'll be fine," Crook responded, and a weary, relieved grin spread across his face. "Nothing's going to happen to the President in front of hundreds of people. It's after the play

I'm worried about. Someone could be lying in ambush in a dark alley or up an unlighted street."

Clapping his hand on the bodyguard's shoulder and squeezing it to reassure him, Faraday steered him toward the stairs. As the two men descended, he promised, "I'll personally ride alongside his carriage when he returns to the White House."

Earl Barlow and Manley Daniels left Taltval's, timing their departure so they would arrive just minutes before curtain time, and went next door. The lobby was practically empty as most of the patrons had already been seated and Barlow had plenty of time to speak at length with one of the ushers. Showing their tickets to the man, Barlow said, "I was told that we would be able to see the President from these seats. Is that true?"

The usher looked at the tickets, then nodded. "Yes, sir, it is. You'll be sitting in the dress circle opposite the President's box. But I'm not promising you'll get to see much of him."

"Why not?"

"Well, sir, if he sits back from the railing, he'll be hidden by the curtains—and he does that most of the time. I've always figured he did it as a courtesy to the folks on stage, so's the audience will watch the performance and not be trying to look at him."

"Oh," Barlow responded, disappointed.

"But, you'll see him when he arrives. And, most likely, he'll step up to the railing and wave to the crowd. He generally does."

"Ah, wonderful, wonderful," Barlow replied. With a smile he thanked the man and began climbing the stairs to the dress circle with Daniels. He did not care whether he could see the President during the performance. Only viewing his arrival was important, for it was then he would best be able to determine the strength of the President's security.

Cole Yeager glanced at Tamara Goodnight, who was seated on his right in the dress circle. The theater lights had not yet been dimmed, and more well-dressed patrons were moving down the orchestra aisles below them or into the boxes around them. Tamara's face glowed with delight as she looked at the audience, her amber eyes coming to rest on one fashionable woman or another and appraising their gowns and jewelry.

Cole, however, could not share in her pleasure. Although he kept a smile on his lips, he was unable to enjoy the evening fully. Like Tamara's, his eyes were wandering, but they kept returning to the vacant double box that had been prepared for the President and his party. From where he sat, he could see the flags hanging against the deep red wallpaper, a framed engraving of George Washington, and the top of a chair, upholstered in dark maroon, that was tucked into the left corner of the box behind the wine-colored curtains. Ever since he had first looked at the presidential box, he felt, for some inexplicable reason, a strange sense of foreboding.

CHAPTER THREE

AT CURTAIN TIME THE PRESIDENT HAD NOT YET ARRIVED AT the theater, but the troupe did not wait for him to appear and began the production. Despite Lincoln's absence, the audience was enjoying the performance. It was a comedy, the actors portraying wildly caricatured figures, but the mood of the theatergoers, celebrating the end of the war, was so jubilant that lines that would not have received a chuckle two months before were now greeted with uproarious laughter.

The play was a little worn. Laura Keene and her theater company had been presenting *Our American Cousin* since 1858. Many of the actors had more than one role, and the actor who played the male comic lead, Harry Hawk, was also Laura Keene's business manager. However, the attractive, gracious British actress had won the hearts of her cast and audiences alike and performed the leading role of Florence Trenchard, which had been created for her, more than a thousand times.

But none of that seemed to matter. The joyful mood of the city, the intimacy of being in the theater, and the fact that so many of the sixteen hundred people in the audience had seen the play before, all contributed to making tonight's performance seem more like a party—a party at which the guest of honor would be the President. Tamara and Cole, of course, had not seen the play before, and the evening was enchanting.

The second scene in the play was well underway when the players on stage suddenly halted in their paces and stepped to the front of the apron. The orchestra, under the direction of William Withers, struck up the first notes to "Hail to the Chief," and the entire audience rose to its feet.

"Oh, isn't it all so wonderful, Cole?" Tamara asked, her eyes glowing with excitement. "The war is finally over, we're seeing a delightful play, and we're in the presence of the President of the United States."

Cole smiled back at her. "And I could add that I am doing it all in the company of a beautiful woman," he whispered.

Standing at attention, he watched as the presidential party entered its box. Not counting the bodyguard, there were four people—an army major and a young woman, plus the President and Mrs. Lincoln. Mrs. Lincoln was smiling broadly, whereas the President seemed somewhat preoccupied. Then Lincoln stepped to the railing at the front of the box, smiled, and waved to the audience with his high hat. The audience applauded appreciatively. Then, gesturing toward the stage, the President indicated that the play should continue.

Picking up the scene where it had been left off, the actor portraying the character of Lord Dundreary spoke his next line. "I caught a window draft, but that was cured by a doctor's draught, which I secured by issuing a bank draft."

"Good gracious," replied Laura Keene as Florence Trenchard, tossing her saucy auburn curls. "What a number of drafts! You have almost a game of drafts."

"Oh, that wath a joke, that wath," Lord Dundreary said, and the audience laughed appreciatively.

Then Miss Keene improvised, "But you need not worry now, for the draft has been suspended."

Few in the audience understood her reference, and there was an awkward pause. When the actor playing Lord Dundreary gave her a puzzled frown, indicating that he did not understand either, the actress looked directly at Lincoln and declared, "Why...anybody can see that!"

Now the audience realized that she was referring to the military draft, and they roared with laughter and applauded her quick and patriotic wit. Smiling delightedly, Laura Keene momentarily interrupted the performance to take a bow. It was all great fun and enhanced the idea that the players and audience were together enjoying a party. With the intimacy even more strengthened, the play continued.

Two people in the audience did not laugh at Laura Keene's quip and were not enjoying themselves. Earl Barlow and Manley Daniels did not share in the party mood and merely stared through the darkened theater at the President's box. Daniels glowered at the President, but Barlow was intently watching Lincoln's bodyguard, who was in the dimly lit corridor outside the box and visible through the door that stood ajar as were all the doors to the boxes. The guard, who had sat quietly for some time, started growing restless. Once or twice he got up to look inside toward the stage, as if bored by his assignment, and returned to his seat. After a few more minutes, he rose, stretched, and looked inside again. Then to Barlow's amazement, the man slipped away from his post, leaving Lincoln completely unguarded. With the doors to the corridor all wide open, Barlow could trace his stealthy progress as the shadowy form made its way to the stairs, hurried down them, and left the theater. The general was incredulous.

Suddenly Barlow found himself, almost against his will, considering Daniels's plan to abduct the President tonight. For one quick moment, he wished he had agreed to it, and he imagined himself slipping through the corridor, stealing through the unguarded door and into the box to capture the President. They would escape into the dark Washington streets before anyone could stop them.

Almost as quickly as the notion struck him, however, he pushed it away. It was an absurd fantasy; Daniels and he could never abduct Lincoln by themselves. More productive than such speculation would be to study Lincoln's security, then devise a careful plan. And if tonight was any indication, the President had no security at all! Barlow felt his pulse quicken in excitement. Capturing Lincoln was going to be as easy as child's play.

Earl Barlow was not the only man to notice the President's security guard leave. Cole Yeager also watched him go, even twisting around in his seat to see if the man actually did go down the stairs or had just repositioned himself for a better vantage point. When he saw the guard leave the theater, Cole looked back at the presidential box to see if Mr. Lincoln had noticed. But the President and Mrs. Lincoln were in the deep shadows of the box, concealed from his view by the heavy curtains that were draped at its edges. Cole felt his uneasiness return.

Tamara Goodnight, sensing Cole's movement in his seat, whispered to him, "Is anything wrong?"

"No," he breathed hastily and shook his head. He smiled reassuringly and turned his attention back to the stage. But the tiny gnawing feeling did not go away, and he kept warily glancing at the presidential box.

At a little after ten, Cole noticed John Wilkes Booth step into the corridor that led to the presidential box. Leaning toward Tamara, he whispered, "I suppose there are certain privileges to being a famous actor."

"What do you mean?" Tamara replied, not taking her eyes from the stage.

Cole pointed toward the presidential box. "Booth just entered the box to be a personal guest of the President," he explained.

Glancing quickly in Lincoln's direction, she then whispered, "Wouldn't you love to be watching the play with the President of the United States?"

Cole looked intently at her. "Right now, I wouldn't trade theater companions for anyone." Gently he touched her hand, and when she did not pull away, he took it in his and continued to hold it.

Tamara smiled shyly and, pressing his hand lightly, looked at the stage.

On stage, the elegant, matronly character of Mrs. Mountchessington fixed Henry Hawk's crude, backwoodsman character with a menacing glare, then hissed, "I am aware, Mr. Trenchard, that you are not used to the manners of polite society." With that, she swept into the wings, leaving Henry Hawk alone on stage.

Since many in the audience had seen the play before, they braced themselves for what they knew would be the biggest laugh in the play.

Hawk did not disappoint them. Putting his hands in his suspenders, he leaned back, peered over his shoulder, then bellowed, "Heh heh. Don't know the manners of good society, eh? Well, I guess I know enough to turn you inside out, old gal...you sockdolagizing old mantrap!"

Laughter burst from the theatergoers. Because he had heard so much about the President's sense of humor, Cole looked over at Lincoln's box to see if the President had moved forward and was laughing. But he never saw the President's face. At that instant he heard an ominous, popping sound, even over the laughter, a sound he had heard many times during the last four years. Startled and confused at hearing that noise in a theater, he rose out of his seat and began looking around wildly. No one else in the audience seemed to have noticed.

Then Cole saw a wisp of smoke float out of the President's box. A second later, John Wilkes Booth climbed onto the railing, then leapt onto the stage floor. One of his spurs caught on a flag, and he fell awkwardly. Cole could tell by the way he landed that he was injured, but many in the audience, recognizing Booth as an actor and believing it to be something new in the play, laughed even louder.

"Cole?" Tamara asked, clutching his arm. It was evident by her tone that she was also confused by what was happening. "What is it? Is this part of the performance?"

"No," Cole replied, his voice tight. "I don't think so."

"Stop that man!" a man suddenly shouted from the President's box. His shout was followed by a woman's shriek.

On the stage, the little comic actor, Harry Hawk, was holding his hat in front of him with both hands, his eyes open wide in surprise and fear as John Wilkes Booth rose to his feet. The actor brandished a knife above his head, glared at the audience, then shouted, "Sic semper tyrannis!"

"My God!" Cole exclaimed, at last understanding what had happened. "Booth has just shot Lincoln!"

"Help...help!" Mrs. Lincoln's voice was a shrill scream that came from the presidential box. Then she babbled, "He said they would take no notice! We were going to Egypt! The Holy Land! Please...someone! Help!"

Cole's seat in the dress circle was not accessible to the stage. Leaping to his feet, he bolted into the corridor and down the stairs, taking them three at a time. As he raced up the side aisle and around the orchestra pit, he saw the orchestra leader jump onto the stage. He also noticed that most of the theatergoers were standing in shock. The confused babble that rang in his ears as he ran by them told him that many people did not know what had just happened.

Cole bounded onto the stage. Two men who had realized what they had just witnessed climbed onto the stage with him. Harry Hawk had disappeared, but lying on the floor boards near the curtains at the wings was William Withers, the orchestra leader. Evidently he had understood what had happened and tried to stop Booth because his shirt front was splattered with blood from a knife wound in his chest. The two men dashed around Withers backstage and began to search in the scenery. One of the men who was wearing the uniform of a policeman shouted, "Stop him! Stop that man!"

Through a gap in the side curtains Cole could see Booth dragging his injured leg and hurrying toward the back door of the theater. Rushing through the curtains, Cole nearly stumbled on the bleeding orchestra leader. The Faraday agent was joined by the two men who quickly identified themselves as A. C. Richards, superintendent of the metropolitan police, and Joseph B. Stewart, a Washington attorney.

"You tend to this man," Cole ordered Stewart. Then he turned to the policeman. "Superintendent Richards, come with me." Cole raced toward the back door and flung it open. Outside in the shadows of the alley, he saw Booth mounting a horse.

"Hold it, you bastard!" Cole shouted, starting toward him with the policeman right behind him.

Booth kicked his mount and slapped the reins against the animal's neck, but the horse was skittish and began turning in tight circles. Seizing the opportunity, Cole dashed toward the assassin, but Booth gained control of the animal just as the agent reached for its bridle. Cole was so agonizingly close that he could feel the leather under his fingertips, but he was unable to grab hold. Booth galloped to the end of the alley, then turned the corner.

Breaking into a run, Cole hurtled out of the alley. Younger and faster than Superintendent Richards, he quickly outran him and left him behind in his pursuit of Booth. Cole chased Booth down F Street for several blocks, cursing the fact that not only was he unmounted, but he had no gun. The actor's horse was fast, and even though Booth was injured, he was a good horseman and held the animal to a gallop. As Booth raced through the muddy streets strewn with slippery, broken cobblestones and threaded his mount around carriages. Cole hoped that the horse would slip or stumble and throw its rider. But the animal moved surefootedly down the street.

Cole saw Booth turn south at the corner of Third Street, but by the time he reached the intersection, Booth was out of sight. An evening fog was rolling in and the street lamps were glowing eerily in the misty night. It's fitting, he thought, that a cowardly attacker would escape on such a night. Cole leaned against one of the lamp posts, gasping for breath. Finally he started the long walk back to the theater, sick at heart and frustrated over his inability to do anything.

While Cole Yeager had gone after the assassin, Tamara Goodnight, obeying her nursing instinct, hurried to the presidential box. As she made her way along the corridor crowded with anxious theatergoers, she saw an army officer, whom she recognized by his insignia as a doctor, pounding on the door of the box.

"I am Dr. Leale!" he called. "Let me in!"

Reaching the door before it had been opened, Tamara heard a muffled voice from inside cry, "Wait a minute. There's a board wedging the door shut."

A moment later the door opened. Tamara entered the box

behind Dr. Leale and saw the major who was part of the Lincoln theater party standing there. He was holding his arm out, and it was dripping blood.

"My arm, Doctor. He cut my arm. Please look at it," he babbled. The young major's eyes wore a dazed, confused expression.

Dr. Leale glanced at the man's arm quickly, then pushed past him. "How is the President?" he demanded.

"But my arm!" the major insisted, turning to follow the doctor with his arm outstretched.

Tamara moved to the major's side and took his arm. "Major, I'm a nurse," she told him. "Let me look at your arm. The doctor should examine the President. Take off your tunic."

As the major removed his jacket, Tamara glanced around the box and saw Abraham Lincoln, bent over in his chair with Mrs. Lincoln trying desperately to hold him up.

"Oh, Doctor," Mary Lincoln cried, her face pitiable, "do what you can for my dear husband. Is he dead? Can he recover?"

While Dr. Leale examined the President, Tamara tended to the major. Taking the silk scarf he had been wearing, she wrapped his wound, then put his other hand on the impromptu bandage. "Hold your hand here as tightly as you can," she instructed him. "We must stop the bleeding."

The major was staring fixedly at the President, his face a mask of desperation. "I couldn't stop him," he mumbled. "I tried to...I tried to grab him, but I couldn't stop him. He came in through that door...I didn't see him."

Suddenly a second man appeared at the railing at the front of the box facing the stage and climbed over the bar. "I am Dr. Taft," he announced. "May I be of assistance, Doctor?"

"Yes, thank you," Dr. Leale replied. "Help me lay the President on the floor."

Seeing the two doctors, Tamara realized that the major and she were in the way. She gently guided the injured, shocked major into a corner and watched as the two physicians worked.

"Have you found a pulse?" Dr. Taft asked.

"No, and he isn't breathing," Dr. Leale answered. Leale took a penknife from his pocket and cut the President's coat and collar away from the shoulders and neck. Then he carefully ran his fingers through the President's hair. "Ah, here it is," he finally said.

"What have you found?" Dr. Taft asked.

"A blood clot behind the ear." He removed the clot, then probed the hole with his little finger. "My God," he said softly. "He has a terrible wound."

"We're losing him, Doctor," Dr. Taft said urgently. "He still isn't breathing!"

Dr. Leale immediately straddled Lincoln's chest, placing his knees on each side of the President's hips. Bending forward, he opened Lincoln's mouth and pressed on his tongue, which had been blocking his windpipe. "Dr. Taft," he said. "I'm going to massage his chest. You raise and lower his arms. We must get some air into him."

Working desperately, Dr. Taft did as he was instructed. Leale began pushing his hands against Lincoln's diaphragm. The President gasped three times, then stopped. Without hesitating, Dr. Leale began mouth-to-mouth resuscitation.

Putting his ear to Lincoln's chest, Taft declared, "He's breathing! He's breathing, and his heart is beating."

"Thank God!" one of the onlookers exclaimed. "You saved him."

Tamara turned away from the scene. She had gazed into the President's face, and she did not share that optimism. She had seen enough men die to recognize the look. Abraham

Lincoln was dying. A moment later, Dr. Leale confirmed her unspoken diagnosis.

"His wound is mortal," Leale said as he stood and looked down at the President. "It is impossible for him to recover."

"Please, let me by," Tamara heard a woman say. She turned to see Laura Keene, whose saucy, bouncy acting had been delighting everyone in the audience only minutes earlier, standing in the doorway. The actress brushed past Tamara into the box and stood beside her.

"Please," the actress repeated. "I have water." She held up a pitcher. Looking down at the President's inert form lying upon the floor, she moaned, "Oh...oh, my God." She sat on the floor beside him, then looked up at the doctors. "Can't I put his head in my lap? Wouldn't he be more comfortable?"

Tamara could tell by the way the President looked that it would not make any difference whether his head was cushioned or not. He was barely breathing and was unconscious. She consoled herself with the thought that he was beyond pain.

"Mrs. Lincoln?" Laura asked, turning her pale, sad face toward the First Lady.

The First Lady was sitting in the chair at the far end of the box, sobbing loudly and uncontrollably. The young woman who had accompanied the major was trying to console her. Tamara had learned in a whispered conversation that she was Clara Harris, and the major was her fiancé, Henry Rathbone.

Receiving no response from the distraught Mrs. Lincoln, Laura Keene tenderly placed the President's head in her lap and began bathing his temples with the water. Tamara knew that the actress's ministrations were accomplishing nothing. But from the many times she, herself, had stood hopelessly by watching good men die on the operating tables of the field hospitals, she knew about the need Laura

Keene felt to do something, anything, even if it was a useless exercise.

"We have to get him to a bed right away." Dr. Leale said.

"Wait," urged Dr. Taft. He pulled a small, silver spoon from his vest pocket and looked around. "Does anyone have any spirits? If we're going to move him, we should fortify his system with a little brandy first."

"I have a flask," someone answered. Tamara glanced toward the voice and noticed that a crowd had gathered in the corridor outside the box. A man was pulling a small flask from his jacket pocket.

"I agree," Dr. Leale replied, "though we should dilute it. I'll hold his head, while you open his mouth. We'll need someone to administer it with the spoon."

"I will," Tamara offered. "I'm a nurse."

With a nod from Dr. Leale, Tamara took the diluted spoonful of brandy and knelt beside Laura Keene. Then she gently slid the spoon past his open lips, poured slowly, and watched him swallow.

By the time Cole Yeager returned to Ford's Theater, everyone inside knew what had happened. As he entered the backstage door and walked onto the stage he saw that all the lights had been turned up to full brightness, and people were milling about on the landings and in the aisles, waiting for word. Many were in tears, some were ranting and cursing, and a few were even smashing the chairs in anger and frustration. There were shouts of "Lynch him!" and "Why didn't someone kill him!" though, of course, there was no one present upon whom they could vent their rage.

"This night is the Rebels' work," someone shouted.

"I say no peace! No peace! We should continue the war until every last one of the vermin are exterminated!"

Cole looked up toward the presidential box. He saw that several men had lifted the President and evidently were about to move him. He searched the group in the box for Tamara and saw even from that distance that her eyes were shining with tears.

"Tamara!" he called.

Hearing her name, Tamara stepped to the rail of the box and looked down.

"Is he still alive?"

"Yes," Tamara called, cupping her hands around her mouth. She looked back over her shoulder to see who was listening, then she added, "but he won't be long. His wound is fatal."

Pointing to the rear of the theater, Cole told her, "I'll meet you at the back stairs."

Tamara nodded, then turned to follow the others out.

"I thank God that we weren't a party to this," Earl Barlow murmured to Manley Daniels. The stunned general had been sitting in his seat ever since the shot had been fired.

"I don't know," Daniels replied. "To my thinking, someone struck a blow for the South."

The general turned to him and demanded in a harsh whisper, "And what will it accomplish? You heard them, how they wish to press even more hardship upon our people."

Daniels sighed in frustration. "Well, what are we going to do now?" he asked.

"I don't know," Barlow admitted, shaking his head slowly. "We have to think about it."

"You two," someone suddenly called. The two men turned toward the voice and saw a man pointing at them. He gestured with his head and told them, "Bear a hand with the President."

"Yes," Barlow answered quickly, getting to his feet. "Yes, of course." The man turned and started toward the presidential box.

Tugging on Barlow's coat sleeve, Daniels sneered and

breathed angrily, "General, we aren't going to help carry that baboon, are we?"

"You want to refuse?" Barlow replied hoarsely, his eyes blazing. "This crowd is-ready for a lynching party, but they have no one to lynch. I don't intend to be their guest of honor, do you?"

Daniels huffed and clenched, then unclenched, his fists. "I guess you're right," he agreed grudgingly. He stood, and the two men hurried to catch up with the man who had summoned them. Reaching the President, Barlow and Daniels joined the dozen others who supported the gravely wounded man as best they could. A couple of soldiers who had been in the audience took it upon themselves to open a path through the stunned and staring crowd as the body was solemnly carried down the stairs.

Once the somber procession was outside. Dr. Leale who was supporting Lincoln's head glanced around the foggy, dimly lit street to determine where they could bring the Wounded President. Everyone had been so shocked by what had happened that no one had thought about where they were going. Suddenly someone cried, "Here! Bring him in here!"

A young man holding a lighted candle was standing on the stoop of Peterson's boardinghouse located directly across the street. The candle flame hobbled as he waved, and Drs. Leale and Taft directed the bearers toward the building.

As the men started up the front steps, negotiating it by hoisting Lincoln's body high for a brief moment, Tamara and Cole came out of the theater, joining the crowd of theatergoers who were following the bearers. They stood under a street lamp watching the tragic proceedings. Tamara pulled her shawl around her shoulders and shuddered, tears streaming down her cheeks. Cole, placing a comforting arm around her shoulder, felt the presence of someone directly behind him. Turning his head, he saw the silver haired Matthew Faraday.

"Mr. Faraday, what are you doing here?" Cole asked.

"It's a long story. I'll tell you later," Faraday replied in a quiet, choked voice. "What happened, Cole?"

The young agent quickly told him, ending his account with his pursuit of the assassin out of the theater. "I followed him for seven or eight blocks, but I was on foot and he was mounted. I didn't have a chance," he concluded, shaking his head sadly.

"At least you were here to try," Faraday said gently. "I didn't even have that chance."

Cole was surprised by Faraday's words. "You weren't supposed to be here, were you?" he asked.

"I promised Will Crook, one of the President's body-guards, that I would be here at the play's end to escort the President home," Faraday told him.

"Then you have nothing to feel guilty about," Cole said, "because the play wasn't over."

"Where was Mr. Lincoln's bodyguard?" Faraday wanted to know. "Where was Parker?"

"Parker? Was that his name?" Cole asked.

Then he sniffed derisively. "I saw him leave the theater about ten minutes before it happened. I thought at the time that his leaving was rather odd." He shook his head angrily. "I should have gone over to stand guard myself."

"Cole, you had no way of knowing what would happen," Tamara said softly. "Don't berate yourself so."

"Miss Goodnight is right, Cole," Faraday told him. "Nor was it your responsibility." Putting a hand on each of their shoulders, he suggested, "Come. Let's go inside and find out what is happening."

They went across the street, and as they made their way up the stairs, several of the men who helped carry Lincoln's body were coming out of the boardinghouse. Barlow and Daniels brushed against Cole, mumbled their apologies, then joined the throng crowding the street between the theater and the boardinghouse. Cole paused and glanced after Barlow. As distracted as he was by what was happening, he still felt something tug at his memory as the man passed him.

Matthew Faraday noticed Cole peering behind him. "What is it?" he asked.

"Do you know either of those men?" Cole asked, pointing to Barlow and Daniels who were now walking under a street lamp.

Faraday looked toward the two men Cole was indicating then shook his head. "No," he replied. "Should I?"

"I don't know," Cole said, frowning. "I think I may have seen the taller one somewhere before, 'but I can't place him."

"Cole, I believe in hunches. If you think those men might have had anything to do with this. I'll stop them right now."

Cole shook his head. "I met a lot of men during the war. If I've seen him before, it must have been then."

Barlow melted into the crowd, and Cole felt Faraday touch his arm. Dismissing the incident, Cole turned to follow him into the house.

Faraday, Cole, and Tamara went into the shadowy hallway and climbed the stairs to a small room at the back of the house. Standing just outside the doorway, they stared in numb disbelief at the President. He was lying motionless at an awkward angle on a bed that was too short for his lanky frame. The pillow beneath his head was covered with blood. The room was lighted with a single, loudly hissing gas lamp that cast an unearthly greenish glow that seemed to intensify the horror.

Suddenly there was a commotion at the front door of the boardinghouse. Mrs. Lincoln, who had been sobbing uncontrollably in the theater, had finally realized that her husband had been taken away. Her face streaked with tears and her dress spattered with blood, she had been led across the street. The stunned, curious theatergoers who had crowded the steps had huddled back to allow her to pass.

"Where is my dear husband?" she shouted wildly. "Where is he? Where have they taken him?"

Kindly people reached out to assist her, but she recoiled violently from them, as if she felt they were trying to manacle her. "What have you done with him?" she screamed, her voice growing louder as she made her way into the building and up the stairs. She finally found the room where the President lay, and she stood beside the bed looking down at her husband, weeping and shaking.

"Oh, somebody, please get Tad," she begged.

"He will live for Tad. He will speak to him; he loves him so."

"Please find some place for Mrs. Lincoln to be comfortable," Dr. Leale spoke up.

Cole understood that the doctor meant he did not want her in the room while they worked on the President, and he and Tamara, escorted the First Lady to a parlor at the front of the house. As he did, two other physicians, Drs. Barnes and King who were attached to the White House, came in and rushed up the stairs to attend the dying man.

Faraday, Cole, and Tamara remained in the house as the death watch continued. Throughout the long night, a steady procession of people—high-ranking generals, cabinet officers, and the Vice President—entered the boardinghouse. General Meigs was stationed at the front door to screen the visitors, allowing in only those with a legitimate right. Secretary of War Edwin Stanton set up his own headquarters in a room next to the one where Lincoln lay dying. While the President was drawing his last, labored breaths, the whiskered, determined Stanton was interviewing eyewitnesses and issuing orders for the capture of John Wilkes Booth.

At about three in the morning, Faraday saw John Parker, the man who was supposed to have guarded the President, standing in the hallway.

"Where were you?" Faraday demanded angrily.

"I was doing my duty," Parker answered.

"Your duty was to guard the President," Faraday grated. "How did Booth get by you?"

"I saw the President safely to his box," Parker replied. "Then, I went next door for a few minutes. Was on my way back when I saw a prostitute working the crowd in front of the theater, so I took her to jail."

"You...you left your post to take a prostitute to jail?" Faraday asked incredulously.

"Yes. After all, I am a Metropolitan policeman. My first duty is to my job...being a bodyguard was only a part-time duty. How is the President, by the way?"

"You sicken me," Faraday hissed. "Get out of here. Get out of my sight before I break every bone in your body."

Waiting with the thousands of people keeping vigil on Tenth Street, Earl Barlow stared at the boardinghouse. He had seen his kidnap plan foiled by John Wilkes Booth, and with it his hopes for a peace treaty that would not destroy the South. But on this misty, cold night Earl Barlow was torn by his emotions.

Few people in the Confederate Army knew the pain Barlow had felt at firing on the Union flag that he had sworn to defend. But when his home state withdrew from the Union, he was forced to make a terrible and difficult decision. Now, despite the fact that Lincoln was the leader of a nation the Confederate officer still considered the South's enemy, he found himself feeling compassion for the man. At one point during the night, he heard one of the doctors state that the wound would most certainly prove fatal, and—to his own surprise—Barlow felt a great sense of sorrow.

Finally the long night passed, and Saturday morning dawned cold, gray, and rainy. Despite the weather, a large crowd kept its silent vigil outside the boardinghouse. Some people had been there all night and still wore the evening clothes they had donned for the theater. So many people had arrived that the street was packed solid with humanity for several blocks in either direction. Many, were weeping, many were cursing, many more were silently praying.

At 7:22, Dr. Leale who had held the President's head throughout the night noticed that Abraham Lincoln had stopped breathing. Dr. Taft placed his hand on his chest, feeling for the President's heartbeat. Dr. Barnes lay his finger on the carotid artery, and Dr. Leale checked the pulse. With a sad nod, the three men then stood, and Dr. Barnes crossed the President's hands on his chest..

Secretary Edwin Stanton, his face streaked with tears, spoke the first words acknowledging the terrible truth. "Now he belongs to the ages," he murmured.

When it was announced to the crowd on the street that the President had passed on, Earl Barlow slowly removed his hat and sighed. He was struck by a profound sense of grief. But he recognized that while part of his sadness was for the man, he was also mourning the death of his plan.

CHAPTER FOUR

THE CITY OF WASHINGTON, WHICH HAD BEEN SO FULL OF JOY over the successful conclusion of the war, was now faced with the most sorrowful of tasks. The red, white, and blue bunting that had so gaily decorated the buildings and lamp-posts of the city was taken down and replaced with black crepe. Citizens who only the day before had gone about their business with a bounce in their step and a sparkle in their eye now moved as sluggishly as if they were living in a nightmare.

Escorted by an army lieutenant and ten privates, President Lincoln's body was placed in a temporary flag-covered coffin, loaded on a caisson, then drawn in a somber parade down Tenth Avenue to Pennsylvania Avenue and on to the White House. Once there, it was taken to the guest room at the northeast corner of the second floor. The body was removed from the temporary coffin and placed on a specially constructed trestle table in preparation for the autopsy.

Secretary of War Edwin Stanton invited certain key people to witness the autopsy. As he told Matthew Faraday when issuing the invitation to him, he believed that such witnesses might prove necessary at the trial, once Booth and his coconspirators—and there was no doubt in Stanton's mind that there were coconspirators—were caught.

The Secretary also knew that Faraday, as a trained observer, would be a good witness. The detective had already performed valuable services for Secretary Stanton during the war, and in this moment of crisis Stanton needed people he could depend upon.

At the appointed time the witnesses arrived at the White House guest room. As Faraday filed into the room with the other somber-faced men Secretary Stanton greeted them at the doorway and directed them to sit in chairs that lined the walls. Walking quickly to his chair, Faraday shivered. The room had been kept cold purposely, but the detective believed that his discomfort came more from the grim nature of the procedure he was about to witness than the temperature in the room. Dr. Barnes, the Surgeon General of the United States, would supervise the work, which would be performed by two pathologists from the Army Medical Museum, Drs. Woodward and Curtis. The three physicians stood next to the President's body. Beside the trestle table near the President's head stood a smaller table that was draped with a white cloth. On it lay an array of surgical instruments and a metal basin. A clerk who would carefully record the proceedings sat at another small table on, the other side of the President's body several feet away.

Lincoln's body was covered with a sheet, which had been pulled down to his waist so that his arms and chest were exposed. Those witnesses who had only seen Lincoln dressed in the baggy dark suits he always wore were surprised at his body. Expecting to see a gaunt, skinny frame, they saw instead powerful arms, a deep chest, and a flat, muscular stomach.

The two doctors began their work, speaking softly in

clinical terms to each other, and the clerk, who was close enough to hear them distinctly, wrote quickly. Dr. Barnes walked over to examine the President's body more closely. "I was amazed at the tenacity for life the President showed," he observed loudly, addressing all present. "Had the wound been anywhere else, he may have survived an injury to which most men would have succumbed."

As Faraday watched from his chair near Lincoln's feet, Dr. Curtis was working around Lincoln's head. The doctor announced in a rich, deep voice, "We have opened the cranium, and I am now removing the brain. I still have been unable to locate the bullet." The clerk dutifully recorded his words.

Then Dr. Curtis carefully removed the brain, and a man sitting two seats away from Faraday gasped. The doctor carried it a few steps to the draped table and began inspecting the gray and white mass of tissue that only the day before had presided over the nation. The room that moments before had been chilly now felt unbearably warm. Faraday noticed another witness remove a handkerchief from his pocket and mop his face. Suddenly a loud clanking echoed in the otherwise silent room as something heavy fell from the brain into the empty basin just beneath it.

"There is the bullet," Dr. Woodward declared, moving to Curtis's side. He reached into the basin, picked up the bullet, and held it high so that all the witnesses could take a good look at it.

"Mr. Faraday," Secretary Stanton addressed him loudly, "did you observe the bullet fall from the President's brain?"

Faraday found his mouth was dry. He swallowed hard and cleared his throat, then said, "I did."

"As you are an expert at such things, would you kindly view the ball more closely and give, for the record, your opinion of its caliber, etcetera?"

Matthew Faraday got up from his chair and walked, over to take the bullet from Dr. Woodward. For a moment he stared at the flattened piece of black lead, no bigger than the end of a finger and seemingly harmless, that had snuffed out the life of a man he considered to be one of the greatest men who ever lived. Sighing softly, he placed the piece of lead in his palm and hefted its weight, then measured its dimension by holding it between his thumb and forefinger. Raising the bullet so all in the room could see it once more, he declared, "This ball was fashioned by hand and has been misshapen by impact. Therefore it is not possible to give an exact caliber. However, without fear of being too far wrong, I would say that its weight and mass are consistent with that of a .44 caliber ball of the type that would be fired by a small pocket pistol, probably a derringer."

"Thank you, Mr. Faraday," Stanton replied. Faraday nodded, placed the bullet in the basin, and returned to his chair. Secretary Stanton turned toward the clerk and went on, "Let it be noted for the record that the cause of death was a grievous wound inflicted by the path of a projectile that struck the President behind the left ear, flattened out as it drove through, and shattered his skull. It then tunneled into the brain, coming to a final resting place behind the right eye. Let it further be noted that this projectile, when recovered from the President's body, was identified by Mr. Matthew Faraday of the Faraday Security Service, a recognized expert in ballistics, as a hand-fashioned ball of approximately .44 caliber, the type normally fired by a pocket pistol such as a derringer. Mr. Faraday, is that consistent with your opinion?"

"Yes," Faraday replied. "Yes, it is."

"Very well, gentlemen, this autopsy is completed," Stanton announced. "We must now allow the morticians time to prepare the President's body for a last viewing by the citizens of this nation. I ask that you all withdraw so that these gentlemen can do their work."

As Faraday rose to leave with the other grim, pale witnesses, Secretary Stanton called to him. Walking toward the stocky, bespectacled man with the flowing whiskers of a biblical prophet, Faraday could not help but notice the lines of strain around his eyes and the determined set to his mouth.

"Thank you for coming, Matthew," Stanton said quietly when Faraday had reached his side. "I know this was an unpleasant task. But if it helps convict Booth and the others, then we shall not have performed it in vain. I'm particularly grateful for your statement regarding the size and caliber of the bullet and the probable weapon that fired it. You may not know this, but as Booth ran from the theater he dropped his pistol, and we have recovered it. It is, of course, a .44 caliber derringer."

"I'm glad I could be of some assistance, Mr, Secretary. I would help in any way I can. In fact, I will put my entire agency at your disposal to find these criminals."

"I appreciate that," Stanton replied, "but I believe that I must turn to the military, not only to find Booth and his accomplices, but to try them as well."

"Try them?" Matthew Faraday frowned. "You mean you intend to subject civilians to a military trial?"

"Yes." Stanton's eyes burned fervently.

"Is that legal?"

The Secretary nodded emphatically. "I have asked Attorney General James Speed for an opinion, and he believes that this was an attempted insurrection, not an assassination. As you know, Secretary of State Seward was also attacked, and Booth left a calling card for Vice President...excuse me, I mean President Johnson yesterday afternoon. I believe that the conspirators intended to kill Lincoln,

Johnson, Seward, and probably others as well." Stanton scowled, and his voice was angry and emphatic as he went on, "Such a broad, coordinated attack on the leaders of our government would certainly be viewed as an attempt to overthrow it. It is clear to Attorney General Speed and myself that we have every legal right to resort to the military to find the criminals and try them for these heinous acts."

"Perhaps you're right," Faraday replied, and his craggy face was grim as he nodded thoughtfully. "How is William Seward?"

Stanton sighed, pushed his spectacles onto his forehead, and wearily rubbed his eyes. "He will recover," he said. "But his son and nurse were wounded more critically than he was, and their recovery depends upon their strength...and what Dr. Barnes referred to a few minutes ago as a tenacity for life." Glancing back at the now- covered body, Stanton took Faraday's elbow and led him from the room. "Come," he said softly, "let's leave this tragic place."

Once outside the White House, Faraday looked up at the second floor. Standing in a window was young Tad Lincoln dressed in his colonel's uniform, staring morosely out toward Lafayette Square, the small park surrounded by an iron fence across Pennsylvania Avenue. Faraday had heard that Tad once locked his father in the park and refused to give him the key, much to the amusement of Lincoln—but to the frustration of those who were waiting to keep appointments with the President. He wondered if Tad was remembering that moment now.

"I imagine that little tyke will recover from this horror," Faraday observed, gesturing toward Tad. "But I'm not so sure about his mother."

Stanton slowly shook his head and stroked his whiskers. "Matthew, I've made no secret of the fact that I have never liked that woman, nor could I understand how Mr. Lincoln could live with her," he said. "But I must confess I now feel great pity for Mrs. Lincoln. She has confined herself to the President's study and is unable even to go into their own bedroom. I'm afraid she will not be able to bear up to the loss and keep her sanity."

Faraday shook his head sadly. "It would be a shame if Tad were denied both his father and mother by the same beastly act." He put his hat on, then reached out to shake Stanton's hand. "If I can be of any further service, Mr. Secretary, you will let me know?"

"Of course, Matthew, of course."

Matthew Faraday learned from the newspapers that it would take an entire week for Washington to say good-bye to the President. Abraham Lincoln's body was scheduled to remain upstairs in the private quarters of the White House until Monday night. He would be kept there to allow the family a period of private mourning. Faraday would learn later that not once during that entire time did Mary Lincoln come to look at his remains. The President would then be taken down to the East Room where high-ranking dignitaries would be invited to view his body. On Tuesday morning he would be on view for the general public. The official funeral was scheduled for Wednesday. After the services Lincoln's body would be transported in a solemn procession from the White House to the Capitol, where he would lie in state in the Rotunda until Friday morning.

It had yet to be decided where the President would be buried. Some, claiming that he belonged to the nation as a whole, felt that it was only proper to bury him in Washington. The governor of Illinois, however, was certain that the President should return to the state where he had built his career as a lawyer and a legislator.

Governor Oglesby happened to be in Washington. He had visited the President just before he left the White House to attend the play at Ford's Theater and had remained during the sorrowful, tragic death watch. He was also one of the few people who was able to see Mrs. Lincoln. The First Lady continued to suffer from shock and refused to see most visitors. However, Governor Oglesby caught her at a moment when she was capable of rational and coherent conversation, Mary Lincoln agreed with the governor. Her husband should return to Illinois.

Determining exactly where in Illinois gave Mary Lincoln more pause. While she favored Chicago, she remembered taking a walk with her husband during a visit to the state capital in

Springfield shortly after the Oak Ridge Cemetery was opened. She specifically recalled him saying that, when his time came, he would like to "rest some place quiet and beautiful...just like this place." This memory, coupled with the aggressive campaigning of a delegation from Springfield, finally persuaded Mrs. Lincoln, and she at last agreed that her husband would be buried in Springfield.

In the dingy room at the rear of the Dunn Hotel, Earl Barlow conducted another meeting one evening with the six men who had come to Washington with him. Barlow, standing next to a small chest of drawers, began to wave his hand at the cigar smoke that filled the small shadowy room. "Would one of you please open the window?" he asked.

"I got a better idea, General," Buford Posey suggested as he rose from where he was sitting on bed and pushed open the grimy window. Grinning, he gestured toward the man who had been sitting next to him. "Let's just throw Dorsey and his cigar out."

The others laughed, Dorsey Evans as heartily as the rest, and Barlow joined them. Then he held up his hand as a signal for quiet, and the laughter died.

"Men, a great deal has happened since we came up here to

embark on our crusade," he began, his blond head turning to look at each of the men as he spoke, "General Johnston has just surrendered, following General Lee's example—" The six men in the room groaned, and Barlow held up his hand once more for silence, "—and of course, Abraham Lincoln has been killed. I've called this; meeting today to decide a further course of action."

"General," Sergeant Evans spoke, up, "I'd do whatever you say. But with Johnston surrendered, what course of action is there for us? What's left to fight for?"

"I'll tell you what is left to fight for," Barlow countered. He picked up a newspaper that was lying on the scarred chest beside him and held it so that all in the room could see the headline. "In all good faith General Johnston accepted the surrender terms General Sherman offered. But I have just learned that those terms have been repudiated in an emergency meeting of the cabinet. The mood of the North, especially with Lincoln dead, is going to be one of revenge. I am afraid the South will face the worst possible future. If we don't have some means of exacting fair treatment from the North, not only will our generation suffer from the loss of the war, but we will have condemned the South for generations to come. One hundred years from now, our great-great-grandchildren will be paying for our defeat."

"General," Dorsey said solemnly, "you don't have to tell us no more. We're with you, no matter what you think we should do." He paused, then asked, "Do you have a plan?"

Nodding, the general replied, "I do indeed."

Manley Daniels, who was leaning against the wall next to Barlow, straightened and snapped his fingers. "We're going to snatch the new President, Andrew Johnson. Right?"

"No, we're not," Barlow said quickly.

"We're not?" Daniels asked in surprise. "But I thought you said—"

"I know what I said," Barlow interrupted, holding up his hand. "But I have just learned some news that has completely changed my mind. Colonel, do you know what has been planned for Lincoln?"

"I don't care what has been planned for that baboon," Daniels snorted. "He's dead and gone, and I say good riddance."

"Yes, I know your opinion of the man," Barlow commented wryly. "But there are twenty-five million other people who don't share that opinion, and, as a result, Lincoln is not quite gone—at least not yet." Barlow pointed to the newspaper still in his hand. "They're going to have a funeral that will cover half this country. He is being placed on a train that is scheduled to visit six states and eleven major cities. All eleven cities are planning memorial services, and you can be assured they will be competing with each other to hold the grandest and most elegant."

"So what has that got to do with us?" Daniels wanted to know.

"Lincoln's train and all these ceremonies will be surrounded by honor guards," Barlow went on as if Daniels had not even spoken. Again he looked at the other five men pointedly to assess their reactions. "Soldiers with unloaded weapons, officers with swords sheathed, caissons with cannon removed, generals with no arms whatever—there will be no security. No one will be armed with loaded weapons. Abraham Lincoln's body will be vulnerable to a well-coordinated campaign."

"Excuse me, General, but I don't understand," Daniels said, shaking his head. "Who would launch an attack against Lincoln now—and why?"

"We will," Barlow answered, shifting his blue eyes to Daniels and looking at him fixedly. "And why...because I intend to steal his body. If we accomplish that, the government will be desperate to have it returned, lest they have another uprising on their hands."

"You mean capture someone who is already dead?" Dorsey asked. His mouth hung open in surprise.

"Yes—and it has a certain macabre beauty to it. If he's already dead; he'll be in no danger because of our actions, nor will we have to make special provision for him or guard him to keep him from escaping."

"Yes!" Daniels cried, snapping his fingers again. "Yes, it's a brilliant idea, General. I see it now!" His hooded dark eyes were alive with excitement as he contemplated the plan Barlow had put before them. "The Yankees would pay almost anything to get that ape's body back, wouldn't they?"

Barlow stiffened at Daniels's words. His blue eyes narrowing, he peered at the colonel. "Pay anything?" he asked. "That's a strange way of putting it. Money isn't the reason we're undertaking this operation. Our purpose is to regain the concessions that the cabinet just repudiated."

"Yes, sir, well, that's what I meant," Daniels said airily, although his eyes continued to glow excitedly. He glanced at Hawkins, Tatterwall, and Chambers, who were lounging in a group against the far wall, and winked mischievously at them.

"Have you figured out yet how to do it, General?" Alan Tatterwall asked.

"Not yet. There are sixteen hundred miles of track to be covered," Barlow explained, "much of it through open country. The journey will take seventeen days at a speed of no more than twenty miles per hour. And, as I said, security will consist only of unarmed honor guards. Surely at some point along the way an opportunity will present itself." He looked at each of the men in turn and smiled. "Rest assured, gentlemen, our beloved South will be accorded right and proper respect once we have completed our mission."

Outside the hotel in an alley beneath the open window a derelict had wandered into the litter- filled passage to sift through the trash barrels when he overheard the conversation. Slipping behind a barrel, he pulled a discarded piece of canvas over himself so he would not be noticed in the dim light coming from the windows. He listened closely as unseen men just a few feet above him plotted to steal Abraham Lincoln's body.

The eavesdropper was frightened. If those men knew he had overheard them, they would surely kill him. And if he went to the police and told them what he had heard, they would pay no attention to him. After all, he was a drunk who made his home in the alleys and under the porches of the city.

Since he would not be believed by the police and would be killed by the conspirators if they discovered him, he decided that the best thing to do would be nothing. Lincoln was dead. What could they do to him now?

He waited very quietly for quite some time, long after the window was closed and there was nothing but silence from the room where the men—whoever they were—had met. Then, with his back aching from the strain of trying to remain motionless for what seemed like an hour, he stood up and took his treasure—a whiskey bottle that an angry wife had discarded while it was still one-third full—and walked away quickly. The best thing he could do would be to get away from here and say absolutely nothing. He intended to forget he had heard anything, and the whiskey would help him do just that.

CHAPTER FIVE

LATE ON THE NIGHT OF APRIL 19, TWO DAYS BEFORE THE funeral train was scheduled to depart, Matthew Faraday heard someone knocking urgently on the pebbled glass of his office door. Pulling his watch from his vest pocket and flipping open the case, Faraday saw it was almost midnight. He briefly considered not responding, but the tragic events of the past few days coupled with the persistence of the knocking made him think better of it. He turned up the gas lamp in the small outer office and opened the door. Standing in the pool of light that spilled into the dark corridor was a man who was clearly down on his luck and badly in need of a shave, a bath, and clean clothes, nervously twisting his battered hat.

Repelled, the detective stiffened. "Yes? May I help you?" he asked, trying to keep the shock out of his voice.

"Yes, Matthew," the man replied with a nod. "I think you can. I sure hope so."

Faraday's piercing blue eyes narrowed as he looked hard at the vagrant. A familiar note in the man's voice touched a memory, and he tried to look through the tangled beard, matted hair, and grime to identify it. The man had also addressed him by his given name, indicating at least an acquaintanceship. Faraday frowned as he spotted a liquor bottle bulging in the man's pocket.

"You don't recognize me, do you, Matthew?" the man asked softly as he smiled self-consciously. "You knew who I used to be," he went on, "but I bear little resemblance to the man whose dinner parties you once graced by your presence."

"Dinner par— Good God, man, who are you?" Then a chill prickled at Faraday's neck, and he knew. "Charles Keith! You are Colonel Charles Keith, aren't you?"

"Yes." Keith laughed bitterly and grimaced. "But as I was drummed out of the service in disgrace...I am no longer called 'Colonel.'"

"Yes," Faraday mused, his craggy face grim. "I remember now. I read something about your trouble." Then, recovering from his shock, he opened the door wider and ushered him into the office.

"Trouble?" Keith muttered, following Faraday. He cackled scornfully and shook his head. "That's being far too kind. At the first battle of Manassas I, as the soldiers so aptly put it, 'showed the white feather.'"

"I can't say I condone what you did," Faraday said honestly. "But you aren't the only one who ran from battle," he added quietly with a hint of sympathy in his tone.

"Oh, you are quite right, sir," he admitted. "Others were frightened during the war, and

others did run from the battlefield...including regimental commanders. But you see, I had the bad luck to do it in the very first battle of the war..." Keith's voice trailed off, and he looked down at his scuffed, ripped shoes for a long moment. "Not only that," he finally went on in a hoarse voice, "but I did it in front of senators, congressmen, newspaper reporters, and the fine ladies and gentlemen of Washington who had come to witness the spectacle. You do remember the event, don't you, Matthew? Just before the battle we had a grand parade through the streets of Washington. Then, in our full-dress uniforms, bright with sash and shining saber, we set out to Manassas to send the Rebels scurrying back South. We were so sure we could end the uprising in one afternoon. That was four years ago. Four years! Who would have thought that so much could happen in four years?"

"Yes, I remember," Faraday replied quietly, recalling the debacle the first battle of Manassas had turned into. And the soldiers were not the only ones to run. Government officials and Washington citizens, who were dressed in their Sunday finest and carried picnic lunches as if they were going to a society fair, had gaily accompanied the army to the battle. But as soon as the soldiers panicked and ran these observers left everything behind in their own desperate flight from the Rebels. It was generally agreed that Charles Keith was the first officer to break and run, abandoning his command. His troops followed him from the battlefield, and their desertion spread to other companies, then to battalions, regiments, and divisions until the entire Union Army was in full retreat.

"I had no training," Keith was saying, shaking his head in disgust. "I was totally unqualified to lead men in battle. I had secured a colonel's commission through political influence. And like everyone else, I looked upon the entire exercise as a lark. Then, when the first bullet whistled by my ear, striking and killing my adjutant and dear friend; I asked myself what I was doing there. Oh, I tried to stay...I willed myself to stay. But the coward inside...made me run screaming from the battlefield."

Faraday was silent, knowing no reply was appropriate or expected.

Keith looked up at Faraday, set his jaw grimly, and went

on. "I would rather have been struck down by one of those balls that day than to have left the field in such utter disgrace. A quick, clean death would have been better than what I have suffered since then. I have lost everything...my fortune, my family, my dignity...and have become the miserable wretch you see now."

Faraday knew that Keith had been a wealthy merchant before the war, and as Keith had reminded him, he had been a frequent guest at his parties. After the Manassas fiasco Faraday had heard that Keith had gone into a decline, but he had no idea of the depths to which the man had sunk. Seeing the man in this condition and knowing the heights from which he had fallen, he could feel only pity for the one they called "the Coward of Manassas." Sighing, Faraday then asked softly, "What can I do for you, Charles?"

Suddenly Keith ran his hand through his matted hair as if he were combing it and straightened his shoulders. Faraday sensed that somewhere in the back of his alcoholic brain Keith remembered that he was once a gracious, well-groomed man.

"It's, uh, not what you can do for me, Matthew," Keith replied self-consciously. "It's what you may be able to do for someone else."

Faraday frowned. "What do you mean, Charles?"

"It's about a plot against Abraham Lincoln. Someone is planning to capture him."

Faraday's eyes opened wide in surprise. Was it possible that there could be anyone in this city who did not know Lincoln had been assassinated? "Charles, surely you realize that—"

"He's dead?" Keith interrupted. "Yes, I know that. Evidently that makes no difference to these scoundrels."

"I'm sorry," Faraday replied, shaking his head in confusion, "but I'm not following you."

"His body," Keith said. "Someone is planning to steal his body."

Matthew Faraday stared at his visitor, who seemed a highly unlikely source of any information. Nevertheless, he decided to hear him out. "Who?" he asked.

Keith shook his head sadly. "I don't know," he admitted. "I only know what I heard last night. I was in an alley, behind a hotel. I, uh, was looking for a place to bed down for the night," he explained, his face filled with shame. "Anyway, I heard several men planning to steal Mr. Lincoln's body from the funeral train."

"Did they say where? Or when?"

"Evidently they haven't yet decided," Keith said, shrugging. "I only know it will occur at some point during the train journey."

"Which hotel were you behind?" Faraday asked.

Keith stared at his threadbare knees, then looked up glumly at his former friend. "I wish I could answer that, Matthew, but I can't," he murmured. "I'm afraid I was inebriated."

"Charles, excuse me for asking this, but, could you possibly have been...that is…"

Keith dropped his head in shame. "You want to know if I was so drunk I imagined this?"

"Yes."

"That's a fair question," he replied and looked squarely at the detective. "In fact, I asked myself that same question this morning, and I almost didn't come to you because, for a while, I wasn't sure. But now I am sure. In the first place, I found a newspaper which carried the funeral itinerary. It is exactly as I overheard, so I couldn't have been making that up. And in the second place, the idea of stealing the President's body would be too bizarre to invent, even for a man in a drunken delirium. No, Matthew, I did not imagine this."

Faraday began pacing the room. "But why?" he asked. "Why would anyone want to do such a thing?"

"If I remember correctly, they intend to hold the body for ransom for what they consider a just treatment for the South."

The agent stopped and looked thoughtfully at his visitor. "I see," he said, nodding. Faraday found himself believing him. He knew only too well that there were fanatics loyal to the South who might hatch such a scheme. "One last question. Why did you come to me? Why didn't you go to the police or the military?"

Keith smiled sadly. "Look at me, Matthew. If you were a constable or an officer, would you believe me? In fact, if you hadn't known me, would you even be listening to me?"

Faraday sighed and looked at the dejected, tragic figure sitting before his desk. "You're right," he admitted. "But tell me, why did you risk saying anything at all?"

"Why?" Snorting, Keith shook his head. "Who knows why? Maybe, in some odd way, I'm trying to make up for what I did. Maybe if I hadn't fled in panic from that battlefield, others would have held. And if we had all held, we might have won that battle and sent the Rebels running. And they would never have been encouraged to make war. Maybe I was, in some way, the cause of four years of suffering for this country and for Mr. Lincoln, who I have heard took the suffering of everyone on his own shoulders." He swallowed hard, his eyes filling with tears. "And maybe I think he should have the right to rest in peace."

Matthew Faraday put a comforting hand on Charles Keith's shoulder. "I think you're being far too hard on yourself, Charles. No one man can bear the responsibility for an entire nation's sorrow—nor should you be bearing such guilt. But I do thank you. And now, please, let me reward you."

"No!" Keith protested, putting up his hand quickly. "If I'm ever going to pull myself out of the gutter-, I must start with one creditable act." Smiling, he stood up and straightened his shoulders. "Perhaps God has given me this chance for that one noble act."

"You know, you may just be right," Faraday said as he guided his visitor to the door. "Don't worry, Charles, President Lincoln's body will make it safely to Springfield. I'll personally see to it."

When Matthew Faraday was admitted to Edwin Stanton's office the next day, he found the energetic Secretary of War dynamically issuing orders to several men crowding the room. Some of the alleged conspirators in the plot to assassinate Abraham Lincoln had been arrested, and there were reports, that John Wilkes Booth had been seen in Maryland.

"I want hourly reports," Stanton was saying to one of the aides bustling around him. "Do you understand? Hourly reports—even if there is nothing to report!"

"Yes, Mr. Secretary," the man promised, then hurried toward the door with the other men.

"Matthew," Stanton called out as the agent stepped into the room. Faraday had to press himself against the door to avoid colliding with the aides. "It's good to see you, my friend. These are trying times, trying times indeed. Nevertheless, I am pleased that you have paid me a visit."

"Mr. Secretary, the country is fortunate to have you in control of the situation at this critical hour," Faraday said.

"I wonder," Stanton mused, stroking the magnificent whiskers that jutted from his chin, "how historians will view me one hundred years from now? I have taken so many liberties with the Constitution that it is as if the document didn't even exist. I am determined to try these conspirators in a military tribunal, but that means I will be suspending many of their constitutional rights. Yet I am absolutely convinced that without swift and decisive action, this country would dissolve into total anarchy. Will history be kind to me, do you think?"

"I don't claim to be a prophet, Edwin," Faraday replied. "But I think your performance during the war has earned you a favorable spot in history, regardless of how anyone may think of how you are handling this."

"Yes, well, if I could speak to the future historians I would merely say to them, 'You did not live through these times and thus could not gauge the peril we faced.'" Then Stanton shook his head, smiled at his guest, and gestured to a chair. "I'm sure you did not come here to listen to me worry about my place in the history books. To what do I owe the honor of your visit?"

"I'm afraid I've learned that there are more foul plans afoot," Faraday said, shaking his head; "Someone is planning to steal the President's body."

During the next few minutes, Faraday told Stanton all that he knew, but he did not reveal the source of his information. When he was through, Stanton was speechless. He stared at him for a long moment, his eyes wide as if he could not believe anyone would attempt something so repellent. Then he pulled off his spectacles and rubbed his eyes wearily.

"Matthew," he finally said. "I can't pull any of my men away from the pursuit of Booth to deal with this. We must locate Booth immediately. The people demand it, and they have a right to demand it."

"I agree," Faraday said, his blue eyes twinkling at Stanton. "That's why I am willing to undertake the job myself. With your permission and indulgence, I will personally guarantee the safe delivery of the President's remains to Springfield."

Stanton replaced his glasses and smiled broadly. "Excellent! I will see to it that you have every legal authority necessary to conduct your business," he promised. "Is there anything else I can do?"

"Yes," Faraday answered quickly. He had been up for several hours after Keith left, carefully, thinking about what he would need should Stanton agree to his protecting the slain President. "I want to establish my headquarters on board the funeral train. That means I'll have to be one of the authorized passengers, but—and this is extremely important —I don't want anyone to know that I am there in any official capacity."

"I agree," Stanton said, his dark eyes narrowing thoughtfully. "In fact, I don't even want anyone to know that such a ghastly plot exists." He shook his head slowly and declared angrily, "There must be no hint of trouble during our nation's time of mourning. Nothing must tarnish the memory of our departed leader."

Faraday was silent for a moment. Then, his voice tight, he murmured, "You have my assurance, Edwin. No word of this will reach the public."

"Good. I don't even want Jonas Ward, my chief of security, to know anything about it—or the real reason you'll be traveling on the train."

"Ward knows me," Faraday cautioned, leaning across the desk, "and he knows my work. He'll definitely be suspicious about my presence."

"Yes, well, do you have any ideas on how to handle that?"

Faraday thought for a moment. "We can tell him that I'm an invited guest because I was a long-time friend and associate of Mr. Lincoln's. He may not believe it, but that's the story we will use."

Nodding, Stanton remarked, "It sounds quite reasonable to me. You have been a guest at the White House, and one of your men was employed as a bodyguard."

"And now, if you don't mind, I would like to examine the guest list."

"It's a large one," Stanton said, picking up a bound document from his cluttered desk and handing it to Faraday. "More than three hundred people are authorized to make the trip."

"Three hundred?" Faraday gasped. "Why so many? That will make the job of guarding the body all the more difficult. Our culprit could be any one of those three hundred."

"No, I don't think so," Stanton declared. "You are free to examine the list very closely, of course. But I think you will find that everyone who has been approved is one hundred percent trustworthy and deserves the honor."

Faraday silently read the list. "Miss Tamara Goodnight," he said aloud, looking up at Stanton. "I see that she is one of the guests."

"Who?" The name was clearly unfamiliar to Stanton.

"Tamara Goodnight," Faraday repeated. "She is the nurse Mr. Lincoln selected to represent all the nurses during the grand victory parade."

"Oh, yes, I remember," Stanton replied. "The head of the National Sanitary Commission personally requested that we invite a nurse to make the trip. But if you think she should not—"

"No, no," Faraday interrupted him, holding up his hand. "I think it is good that she be allowed to go. In fact, I intend to confide in Miss Goodnight. She will be the only person on that train who will know the true reason for my being there."

"Do you think that's a good idea?" Stanton asked, his voice tinged with concern. "Do you know this woman?"

"I met her only recently," Faraday admitted. "But I was most favorably impressed with her. I think she will do nicely."

"Very well. I'm sure you know your business well enough

to judge whom to confide in. But charge her with the responsibility of remaining silent about this. Remember, I do not want anyone to be aware that this terrible threat even exists. And once the operation is over and the President is safely and reverently buried, I do not want anyone learning that the danger ever existed. If the public knew, given the present mood of the country, I fear all law and order would break down."

"I promise you, no one will ever know," Faraday vowed as he rose to his feet. Reaching across the desk, he shook Secretary Stanton's hand, then turned and hurried out of the room.

As General Earl Barlow climbed the front steps of the Dunn Hotel, he glanced at the black bunting draped across its facade and shrugged. The hotel clerks were all wearing black armbands, and Barlow had decided to avoid calling attention to himself by wearing a black mourning ribbon pinned to his jacket lapel. Striding across the lobby, he saw Daniels and his three men lounging on the worn upholstered chairs reading newspapers. Daniels looked up, and Barlow lay his finger aside his nose to signal that he wished a meeting. Then by holding up two fingers, he indicated that they should meet him at two o'clock. Daniels nodded imperceptibly and raised his newspaper as Barlow continued across the lobby into the corridor that led to his room.

Once inside, Barlow scowled at the stale air and went to the window to open it. As he raised it, he noticed a man poking in the trash bins and litter in the alley outside, and a chill ran up his spine. He realized he had better be careful in conducting his meetings from now on because he was certain that anyone in that alley could hear everything that was said. Then the man picked up an almost empty bottle, raised it to his lips, and drained it. Barlow almost laughed out loud in relief. A drunk, Barlow knew, would not be interested in their patriotic plots. Nevertheless, he quietly closed the window.

Turning toward the bed, he strolled over to it and sat down heavily. Patriots. *Is that an accurate description of us?* he thought wearily. He had asked himself more than once if what they were doing was sheer folly. Patriots.

Certainly Colonel Manley Daniels was patriotic to the cause he believed in. He had personally raised and equipped the regiment he commanded during the war. Though Daniels had a cruel streak Barlow found distasteful and was short-tempered, domineering, and self-centered, he accomplished what he wanted. If he could convince Manley Daniels that they both wanted the same thing, Barlow thought, then he could rely on him completely.

But the best man in the entire group, as far as Barlow was concerned, was Sergeant Dorsey Evans. Loyal almost to a fault, Dorsey would be the man the general could count on the most.

Private Buford Posey was another good man. Buford had come along because Dorsey asked him. And Dorsey had come because Barlow asked him.

Daniels had brought three men of his own—Pete Chambers, Lee Hawkins, and Alan Tatterwall. Barlow sighed and shook his head. Frankly, these were not the sort of men he would have selected to surround himself with, but the mission he had chosen to undertake was difficult and dangerous. He would need the most skilled and daring men he could find, and, he told himself, you did not find such men at a Sunday-school picnic.

A knock at the door startled him from his musing. He looked at his watch and saw it was time for the meeting. Composing himself, he stood and crossed the room to let the others in.

"General, why are you wearin' that there mournin'

ribbon?" Lee Hawkins asked, his pugnacious jaw jutting in derision.

Barlow walked over to the scarred chest and picked up a box, then held it out toward the men. "We're all going to wear one," he replied.

"No, sir, not me," Alan Tatterwall insisted, holding up his hand.

"Oh, yes you are," Barlow countered dryly. "Or you can just walk out of this room right now."

"General, you know me," Dorsey said, taking one of the ribbons and pinning it onto his jacket. "You tell me to wear the damned thing, and I'll wear it. But I don't like it no more'n Tatterwall does, and I'm wonderin' why you're askin' us to do it."

"Because nine out of ten people are wearing them right now," Barlow said. "The ones who aren't are standing out and attracting attention. In some cases, they've even been jumped on and beaten up."

"I can take care of myself if any Yankee wants to try somethin'," Tatterwall boasted.

"I've no doubt that you can," Barlow retorted, "but I'm not worried about that. What I am concerned about is your standing out in a crowd. Right now soldiers are pulling people off the street for any reason whatsoever. Why, if someone so much as whispers an unpatriotic sentiment, he's suspect. They're not just looking for Booth, they're looking for anyone else who might have been involved with him. I don't want one of you picked up for the wrong reason and then let the authorities, by accident, stumble onto what we've planned."

"Put on the ribbons," Daniels ordered, reaching into the box and taking one. The others immediately followed suit.

Barlow smiled and nodded at Daniels.

"General, do we have a plan?" the colonel asked.

"Yes," Barlow replied. "I've just learned that the train will be leaving Washington early tomorrow morning and is scheduled to arrive in Baltimore at ten o'clock. There won't be an opportunity for us to act between Washington and Baltimore, but there will be after the train leaves Baltimore. Dorsey, Buford?"

"Yes, sir," they answered as one.

"You two and I will ride to Baltimore tonight, so that we can be at the depot when the train arrives. That will be our first opportunity to have a good look at things, to make certain that they haven't pulled any surprises on us. If everything is as expected, we'll ride quickly to the switch house at the junction of the Westminster spur." The general shifted his focus. "That's where you, Colonel Daniels, and the others will be waiting, after taking care of the switchman or anyone else who might be there."

"How far is that from Baltimore?" Daniels inquired.

Barlow pulled a railroad map out of his jacket pocket and spread it on the bed. As the men crowded around to watch he traced the route with his finger. "I estimate that it's about five miles away—close enough that we can get to it quickly, but far enough to be out of the congestion of the city. By throwing the switch there, we can divert the train onto the Westminster spur-line. That will cause them to stop, and then we'll board the special funeral car and take Lincoln's body."

Daniels studied the map for a few moments, then looked at Barlow and asked, "Who will be guarding the body?"

"Two generals," Barlow answered with a broad smile. "Neither of them armed."

"How will we get away?" Dorsey wondered. Looking at each man in turn, Barlow explained carefully, "I plan to cut the telegraph wires leading into and out of the switch house, so that no one aboard the train will be able to send a telegram. In addition, we'll damage the track and make it impossible for the train to either proceed forward to Westminster or back up to Baltimore. Of course, there won't be any horses on the train, so the passengers will have to send someone on foot to carry the news of what happened. That will give us at least an hour's head start. Since we'll all be on horseback we'll be long gone before they even start their search."

Daniels smiled. "General, that's brilliant! By this time tomorrow night, the Yankees'll be ready to give us anything we want."

"All we want is just and fair treatment," Barlow reminded him.

"Sure, General, that's what I mean," Daniels said quickly, and he smiled knowingly at Tatter- wall, Hawkins, and Chambers—the three men standing nearest to him. "That's exactly what I mean."

That same afternoon in her room at the National Hotel, Tamara Goodnight was busily packing her things in preparation for the trip on the funeral train when she was surprised by a knock on her door. Laying her green velvet gown on the bed, she went to open it and was startled to see Cole Yeager towering in the doorway. "Cole, hello."

Tamara had seen him twice since the tragic night Lincoln was shot before their eyes. The handsome former colonel had taken her to dinner on Monday evening, and on Tuesday morning they had joined the throng of mourning Washingtonians who filed past Lincoln's bier in the East Room of the White House. In both instances Cole had written notes extending gracious invitations and had them delivered to her room. She had accepted both in writing and was deeply touched by these gentlemanly gestures and the courtly way he treated her when they were together. As a result, his sudden appearance in her doorway was quite unexpected.

"Tamara," Cole said warmly, his blue eyes twinkling as he smiled. "Matthew Faraday asked me to deliver this to you personally." He had taken an envelope from his jacket pocket and was holding it out.

"Thank you," she replied, taking the note. "Is he expecting an answer right away?"

Cole nodded. "Yes, in person. At least, that's what I gather. You see, I received a note from him as well, asking me to bring you to his office."

Puzzled by the strange request, Tamara opened the note and read.

DEAR MISS GOODNIGHT:

You are to be congratulated! An invitation to ride on board the funeral train of Abraham Lincoln is indeed an honor. By your presence you will represent all the brave women who, like yourself, served our nation so nobly in the hospitals and aid stations of the war so recently won. It is most fitting and proper that you should be a part of this historic event.

And now, dear lady, I wish to ask if you are prepared to make a further contribution to your country and to the preservation of the dignity of the man we are honoring. I have been empowered by Secretary of War Stanton to solicit your help on a matter of grave importance. If you are willing to offer your services, please accompany Cole Yeager to a meeting in my office at four o'clock this afternoon.

SINCERELY
Matthew Faraday

TAMARA WAS EVEN MORE MYSTIFIED than before, although

now her curiosity was also piqued. "What's all this about, Cole?" she asked.

"I honestly don't know," Cole admitted. Smiling at her, he added, "But I hope you're as curious to find out as I am."

"I certainly am. Just let me get my wrap," Tamara answered, returning his smile.

Hurrying down the stairs and out of the hotel, Cole and Tamara hopped into one of the hackney cabs that lined the curb, and Cole directed the driver to take them to E and Tenth streets. When the cab halted in front of the building that housed the Faraday Security Service at a few minutes before four, the two of them looked sadly across the street at the bunting-draped facade of Ford's Theater. The building was closed, its doors padlocked, its windows boarded shut, and soldiers stood solemnly guarding the front.

At dinner on Monday night Cole had told Tamara what had happened to the theater. He had learned that people who were seeking relics had stolen almost all the physical evidence that, should have been preserved for the trial of the assassins. One of the stagehands had found the piece of wood Booth had used to jam the corridor door shut, and he had cut it into small sections to sell to the souvenir hunters. The presidential box was in ruins. Large pieces had been cut from the draperies and long strips of wall paper had been peeled away.

Tamara's amber eyes were mournful, and she shivered slightly as she stepped down from the carriage. "Are you all right?" Cole asked.

"Yes," she replied. "Just a slight chill." Pulling her cloak about her, she took Cole's arm and went into the building. At precisely four o'clock Cole knocked on the pebbled-glass outer door,

and Matthew Faraday, greeting them warmly, led them into his office.

Hot, fragrant coffee and a plate of delicate pastries sat on a tray on Faraday's desk. Cole escorted Tamara to a chair, then went to the other chair, while the silver-haired detective moved behind his desk. He poured coffee for each, offered them pastries, then sat across from them to explain why they had been summoned.

"I'm sure you are wondering what sort of service I am asking of you," Faraday began, his craggy face grim.

"Yes," Cole replied and turned to Tamara. "I think I can answer for both of us and say that we are quite curious."

Faraday looked at each of them intently as if he were trying to make up his mind about them one more time. Then he spoke very carefully. "Incredible as it may seem, I believe someone is plotting to steal Abraham Lincoln's body between now and the time it is buried in Springfield, Illinois."

"What?" Cole cried, his face aghast. "For what purpose?"

"It may be hard for us—the sane—to fathom the purpose of an insane plot," Faraday replied, "But I believe the plotters intend to take Mr. Lincoln's body and hold it hostage until they are satisfied with the terms of the South's surrender."

"Then it's a plot of the Confederate government?" Cole asked.

Shaking his head, Faraday replied, "No, I don't think so."

Tamara sat forward in her chair. "Do you think it might be someone who's in league with Booth?"

"No, I don't think that either," Faraday told her. "I believe it's the desperate plan of a group of disgruntled Southerners who see this as a last chance to have an effect on the outcome of the war."

Tamara shuddered. "It would be awful if something happened to the President's body now."

"I agree," Faraday replied, nodding his head solemnly. "And it's for that reason that I take this plot seriously. For even if the motive behind it is insane, the effect would still be devastating to a nation that needs this funeral—not only, to say good-bye to our martyred President, but also to say good-bye to their own loved ones who fell during the war. If something were to happen that would disturb this mourning process now, it would take years for the wounds of this nation to heal."

"Ironically, if the plotters are successful, they might well have just the opposite effect of what they're seeking," Cole pointed out.

"I believe that too," Faraday said.

"I suppose Stanton is turning out the entire army to keep it from happening," Cole said as if he were thinking aloud.

Taking a swallow of his coffee, Faraday studied Cole and Tamara over the edge of his cup. "No," he finally said. "He is taking no action at all."

"What?" Cole exclaimed.

"Why?" Tamara added. "I don't understand."

"Stanton wants absolutely no hint of trouble. He wants nothing to tarnish the memory the people have of Abraham Lincoln." Faraday paused meaningfully. "And I agree with him."

"But surely," Tamara began, her eyes narrowed anxiously, "something is going to be done to keep this from happening?"

"Oh, yes," Faraday assured her. "And we are going to do it. That is, if you are willing to participate."

"Yes, yes, I'll do anything you ask," Tamara promised.

"What is our plan?" Cole asked.

Faraday smiled. "I knew I would be able to count on the two of you," he said. Setting down his cup, he leaned back in his chair. "Tamara, you and I will be on board the funeral train for the entire trip. So will Jonas Ward, Stanton's chief of security, and several high-ranking members of the military.

But—and this is important—they do not know of the plot, and they are not to be told or involved. Among all the passengers, only you and I will know. I'm involving you because I want Cole to be able to have someone else to get in touch with in the event he can't reach me. Of course, there will also be other, more specific things I'll be asking of you as well during the trip," Faraday added.

Tamara nodded. "Since you are the security expert, Mr. Faraday, I won't question your judgment."

"Fine," he said, smiling. Then he turned to Cole. "I want you to travel ahead of the train, arriving in each city well before we are scheduled to be there," he told him. "You are to keep your eyes and ears open, but don't let anyone know, what you are doing."

"Very well," Cole agreed.

"Before the two of you leave, I will provide both of you with a code. Cole, either Tamara or I will check at each stop for your coded telegraph messages, and you check for messages from us. We must keep in constant touch." He looked at each of them, adding, "I wish I could be more specific on who or what to look for, but the truth is, I don't have the slightest idea. I know only that the danger exists, but I don't know from where it will come."

Cole smiled. "Well, I've had a few years of looking out for danger from all corners," he reminded Faraday.

Faraday returned his smile. "You certainly have, and I'm counting on that to help you out. I believe in instinct," he added. "If something doesn't seem quite right to you, then chances are it isn't right. Don't waste time thinking about it. If you find yourself in that sort of situation, act."

"Don't worry, I will," Cole promised.

Faraday paused and looked intently once more at Cole and Tamara, searching their faces. At last he said, "I have a feeling that the events of the last few days have caused you two to develop a rather strong friendship. That's all very good, but I want you to say good-bye to Tamara as soon as this meeting is over, because I want you to leave for Baltimore as soon as possible. I want you there before the funeral train arrives tomorrow."

"Of course, Mr. Faraday," Cole replied.

"And Cole," Tamara said softly, "be careful."

Cole smiled at her. "I haven't lasted this long by being careless."

"Now," Faraday began, "this is what I want you to do."

CHAPTER SIX

AT SIX O'CLOCK ON THE MORNING OF FRIDAY THE TWENTY-
first of April, Matthew Faraday, Tamara Goodnight, and
three hundred carefully selected passengers stood waiting on
the Baltimore and Ohio station platform beside the funeral
train. Among the senators, congressmen, and dignitaries
making the journey were the President's two brothers-in-
law from Springfield; two first cousins of Mrs. Lincoln; Dr.
Phineas Gurley, a pastor of the Presbyterian church; Dr.
Brown, the embalmer; and Thomas Pendel, the White House
doorkeeper who had put young Tad Lincoln to bed on the
night his father was assassinated.

A cold drizzle was falling, but the overhanging roof of the
platform sheltered Tamara, Faraday, and the other passengers as they stood waiting for the hearse that bore the slain
President's body and its escort. A few minutes earlier, in a
discreet but solemn ceremony, a small casket had been
loaded onto the funeral car.

"What is that?" Tamara had whispered to Matthew Faraday. "It looks like a coffin, but it's much too small to be the
President's."

"It is a coffin," Faraday explained. "But it bears the President's son, Willie. It was the family's wish that Willie be returned to Springfield to be buried with his father."

Tamara nodded slowly. "Oh, yes, I remember now when he died. It was very sad."

"Some people say that after Willie died, the laughter left the White House," Faraday told her. "Lincoln loved all his sons, of course, but I've always thought he was particularly close to Willie."

The engineer had already built up the steam pressure in the locomotive as it waited with its string of nine cars for the somber cargo. The relief valve opened and closed rhythmically to vent excess pressure, producing what Faraday thought was almost a sobbing sound.

The 4-4-0 Baldwin engine had been selected because it was the most beautiful locomotive on the Baltimore and Ohio Line. To prepare it for the solemn occasion, it had been cleaned meticulously, its brass fittings polished to a high shine, and then heavily draped in black crepe. The American flags fitted to the top of the cowcatcher where they protruded on either side of the boiler provided the only touch of color. On the front of the boiler was a wreath that encircled a large, black-bordered picture of the President.

Faraday heard the heavy boom of a distant cannon, and he knew that sound signaled the departure of the funeral-cortege from the White House to begin its stately procession up Pennsylvania Avenue toward the depot. When he had ridden to the station at dawn, he had not been at all surprised to see that despite the early hour, thousands of people were standing on each side of the avenue, weeping and waiting to say one last good-bye.

Matthew Faraday decided that before the cortege reached the depot he would examine the funeral car to determine whether security would be difficult to maintain. He invited

Tamara to view it with him. The two of them made their way along the crowded platform toward the rear of the train, Tamara holding the skirt of her dark gray traveling suit close to her to prevent it from being stepped on in the crush of people.

The car—the last of the nine cars—had been specifically built to be used by the President of the United States during his official travels. As fate had it, this would be the first and only time President Lincoln would ride in the car.

The original design called for the car to be divided into three sections—a bedroom, sitting room, and dining area. For this somber journey, the sections had been converted. The front section now provided seating for the honor guard; in the larger, middle section stood the bier on which the President's coffin would lie; and the rear section, the smallest of the three compartments, housed the coffin bearing Willie. The middle section was stark and empty, and just behind the partition that separated it from the rear section, Faraday and Tamara could see that Willie's coffin was already in place.

The inside walls, floor, and ceiling of the car, which had been covered in a rich, maroon tapestry, were now veiled by heavy black drapery while on the presidential bier was a black pall fringed with knotted tassels. Next to the catafalque were two empty chairs, one on each side. During the trip one of these chairs would be occupied by Admiral Charles Davis, representing the navy, and the other by General Edward Townsend, who would represent the army.

"What are you doing in here, Mr. Faraday?" a powerful voice demanded.

Faraday turned and saw a middle-aged, heavy-set man standing in the doorway. Jonas Ward, Edwin Stanton's chief of security, had just entered the car.

"Hello, Mr. Ward," Faraday replied lightly, ignoring the

man's overbearing tone. "Miss Goodnight and I were just viewing the funeral car. It's really quite beautiful."

"Yes, it is, isn't it?" Ward murmured. Then he smiled at Tamara. "I don't believe I have had the pleasure, Miss Goodnight."

Faraday introduced Tamara, explaining that she was a nurse who would be riding on the funeral train as a representative of the Sanitary Commission.

"It's good to have you with us," Ward remarked to Tamara. "And you, Mr. Faraday—I understand from the Secretary that you are making this trip because you are an old family friend of the Lincolns?"

"I don't know as I would say I was an old family friend," Faraday said. "But when Mr. Lincoln was a lawyer in Illinois, I did some investigating for him, and after that a friendship developed between us."

"I see. You aren't still investigating for him, are you?"

Faraday gave the man a puzzled look. "What do you mean?"

"It's no secret, Mr. Faraday, that you have performed some services for Secretary Stanton in the past, and I'm certain that those were authorized by the President personally. I would not want you to get the idea that any such services are required of you on this trip. All security arrangements are being handled by the Department of State and the Department of War. You do clearly understand that, don't you?"

"Yes, of course," Faraday said, Jonas Ward stroked his chin and looked at Faraday for a long moment. "Good, good," he finally said. "As long as you realize that you are on this train as a mourner and nothing more, there will be no problems between us."

"Don't worry, Mr. Ward. I anticipate no such problems whatever."

The muffled thump of drums grew louder, signaling the approach of the funeral procession. Ward leaned over to look through the car's window. "The cortege should arrive at any moment," he murmured. "I had best get onto the platform to see that everything is handled properly." He started toward the door, then turned back to Faraday and Tamara. "I must ask you to leave because while the President's coffin is being loaded onto the train only the honor guard will be allowed in the funeral car."

Tamara stared at him in surprise. "You mean not even the family members will be present?" she asked.

Ward shook his head slowly. "Except for a couple of cousins, there are no family members making this trip, Miss Goodnight. Since the President was shot Mrs. Lincoln hasn't attended a single official function. She has kept herself closeted in his study throughout all the services."

"Oh, the poor woman," Tamara murmured. "Has anyone tried to talk to her, to comfort her? Has anyone asked her if she would like to be on the train?"

"Oh, yes, she has been asked several times if she would like to accompany the President, but she has refused every offer. I must say, it's causing no small amount of talk. Some people believe her refusal is very callous, as if she had no feelings at all over the fact that her husband is dead."

Remembering the hysterical woman she had tried to comfort at the Peterson boardinghouse, Tamara stiffened in anger. "How foolish of anyone to think such a thing!" she cried, her amber eyes narrowed. "It's quite obvious that her pain is very deep. Perhaps not going to any of the funeral ceremonies is the only way she can cope with her grief."

"What about Robert?" Faraday asked. "Will he miss the funeral, too?"

"Robert will not be on the funeral train because he has

decided to stay in Washington and look after his mother," Ward replied. "But he will take a later, faster train and be in Springfield for the entombment."

The sound of the drums had grown so loud that it was clear the cortege had arrived in the station. Faraday took Tamara's elbow and ushered her to the door of the car. "Come, we'll let the honor guard do their work now." As they stepped down onto the platform, Faraday added under his breath, "While I do mine."

"What are you going to do?" Tamara asked, looking pointedly into Faraday's sharp blue eyes.

Glancing around to be sure that no one was within earshot, he whispered, "I'm going to send a wire to Cole in Baltimore telling him that we're about to depart and that everything is okay so far. Wait here. I'll be back in a few minutes." Faraday hurried to the telegraph office inside the depot to send the message. When he returned, Tamara and he watched the cortege move onto the platform. Then Dr. Phineas Gurley, the pastor, stepped to the head of the coffin to offer a prayer while everyone present—those who would ride on the train as well as those who would remain in Washington—removed their hats and bowed their heads.

"Watch over this sleeping dust of our fallen chief magistrate as it passes from our view and is borne to its final resting place in the soil of that state which was his abiding and chosen home," Dr. Gurley prayed.

Silently Faraday offered his own brief player asking for help in ensuring that Abraham Lincoln's body would be delivered, undisturbed, to its final resting place.

As soon as Dr. Gurley uttered, the last syllable of his prayer, the engine's bell began to clang. The sound came so quickly that Faraday suspected the engineer had been irreverent enough to have his hand on the cord throughout the prayer. Smoke began belching from the wide mouthed stack even as the conductor and other officials began quickly ushering the passengers aboard. Moments later the funeral train inched away from the platform and out of the depot.

"Oh, Mr. Faraday, look!" Tamara called as she gestured toward the window. "Who are those soldiers?"

"It's a Negro regiment," he replied softly, a sad expression on his lean face. "They weren't allowed to enter the depot, so they chose to pay their respects this way."

The black soldiers were lined up alongside the tracks, standing rigidly at attention, their grief evident on their tear-stained faces. As the train passed the soldiers, Faraday thought that he had never seen a more moving tribute.

Although it was just drizzling in Washington, it was raining quite hard in Baltimore. But the inclement weather had not discouraged the thousands who wanted to pay tribute to the President. Clamping his hat down on his head and buttoning his greatcoat tightly around him, Cole Yeager stepped out of the telegraph office and shook his head in amazement. Not only was the depot platform crowded, but people lined both sides of the track for as far as he could see.

This is ironic, he thought. Before the war Baltimore had been such a hotbed of secessionism that the newly elected Abraham Lincoln had to be sneaked through the city on his way to Washington. Now every face was touched with grief. It was not only an impressive sight, but a vivid example of the hold the President had on the hearts of the people.

Cole stuck his hand into his deep pocket, and his fingers closed around the telegram he had just been given. In Matthew Faraday's code, which Cole had quickly memorized, the detective had informed his new agent that Lincoln's body had safely reached the depot and that they were on their way to Baltimore.

Cole had left Washington before midnight and ridden north very slowly along the Baltimore and Ohio tracks. He had stopped at every trestle, crossing, and switch plate and examined each one carefully by lantern light to make certain that no one had tampered with them. A pilot engine, traveling a half hour ahead of the funeral train, would sweep the track, but Cole realized that anyone interested in derailing the funeral train would have time to set up the appropriate mechanism after the pilot engine had passed. When he reached the Baltimore city limits at daybreak, he breathed a sigh of relief because he had found nothing to indicate that anyone was planning any sabotage along the entire route. Nevertheless, he continued his scrupulous examination until he was in the depot. Stabling his tired horse at a livery adjacent to the rail yard, he had made his way to the depot telegraph office.

Now he strolled among the still growing crowd gathering to await the funeral train's arrival, casually studying the people. He could not help smiling when he noticed energetic entrepreneurs hawking their wares to the waiting throng. Young boys were doing a brisk trade selling black crepe rosettes and small photographs of Lincoln. A half dozen preachers were also taking advantage of the captive audience by delivering loud, impassioned sermons. The preachers seemed to have chosen a common theme, revolving around the fact that Lincoln had been assassinated on Good Friday, and drew parallels between Christ's crucifixion and the President's martyrdom.

Amid the varied smells of the crowd, an appetizing fragrance reached the agent's nostrils. Since Cole towered above the throng, he readily spotted a vendor who had set up a cart on the platform and was brewing and selling hot coffee. He worked his way over to the man, bought a cup, and continued his scrutiny as he drank it. As he ran his eyes over the unfamiliar faces, he recalled the end of yesterday's conversation with Matthew Faraday.

"You're obviously a lot more experienced in this sort of work than I am," he had told the detective. "Do you have any hints about what I should be looking for?"

"Only one suggestion," Faraday had replied, smiling. "Don't look for anything." When Cole's face registered his surprise, Faraday laughed and went on, "I know that sounds foolish, but it's the truth. If you're consciously looking for something out of the ordinary, you're going to miss it. You'll either convince yourself that something is wrong when it isn't, or you'll convince yourself that everything is fine when it's not quite as it should be. The best thing to do is not to look for anything in particular. Make your mind a clean slate. Let your eyes sweep naturally across whatever you are studying. If something registers on that clean slate, then consider investigating it."

Huddling into his coat against the cold, steady rain, his hands relishing the heat from the steaming cup, Cole thought of Faraday's instructions and made his mind as clean a slate as possible. It seemed to be working, for the images he was seeing raised no alarm.

He saw umbrellas...so many they seemed to meld together to form a single large canopy covering the thousands who were waiting patiently. He saw children standing silently at the skirts of their mothers, looking on with big eyes and indelibly fixing the scene in their minds to form memories that would be shared with their grandchildren in the next century. And he saw Earl Barlow, leaning against a rain-slicked post.

At first the man's face and blue eyes peering out from under his broad-brimmed gray hat merely tickled his memory. Cole blinked and shook his head. He turned to put his coffee cup down on the vendor's cart, and it was then that he recalled where he had seen him before. The first time was several years ago at Spotsylvania, when he was arranging to exchange a Confederate general for some Union prisoners. That general had been Earl Barlow. Cole also remembered the last time he had seen Barlow. He had brushed by him as he was entering the Peterson boardinghouse across from Ford's Theater on the night Abraham Lincoln was assassinated.

Cole worked his way through the crowd until he reached the General's side.

"Good morning, sir," Cole said pleasantly. "We meet again."

Barlow looked up at him, his face blank under the dripping brim of his hat. "I beg your pardon, sir, but you've mistaken me for someone else. We've never met."

"But of course we have," Cole replied. "Surely you remember me? I am Colonel Yeager, formerly of General Grant's staff. And you are General Earl Barlow."

"I'm honored that you believe me to be a general, but you are mistaken." Barlow nodded. "If you'll excuse me, sir," he said, then turned and slipped into the crowd.

Frowning, Cole watched as General Barlow made his way toward the other end of the platform. He was certain he was not mistaken. And now that the war was over, he could not understand why Barlow would not want to be recognized.

Was this the kind of thing that should register on the clean slate Faraday spoke of? Perhaps. The exchange had certainly been troubling to him.

Suspicious, Cole pushed his way through the crowd, following Barlow as best he could. From a distance he watched the general approach two men, stop to speak with them briefly, then continue toward the end of the platform. Something in the man's manner made Cole decide to keep

Earl Barlow in sight for as long as possible— hopefully until the funeral train had left Baltimore without incident.

Stooping, slightly, Cole slipped among the crowd, ducking, behind people in an attempt to conceal himself from the general, who looked back over his shoulder every so often. Then Barlow abruptly picked up his pace, and Cole suspected he knew he was being tailed. He was certain of it when the general suddenly darted across the tracks and began running toward the freight-switching yard—a rabbit's warren of standing boxcars and half-assembled trains. Realizing that Barlow could easily elude him in such a maze, Cole picked up his own pace, trying to close the gap between them.

As Cole rounded a car he noticed that at the farthest end of the yard several men were working around a freight train, apparently preparing it for departure. Barlow changed direction and started toward it, and Cole followed.

"General! General, wait!" he cried as he ran. "I just want to talk to you!" But Barlow neither slowed nor replied. Maybe he didn't hear me, Cole thought, but he doubted it. Why would a man who had been waiting patiently for the funeral train to arrive leave so abruptly as soon as he approached him?

Cole was within fifty feet of his quarry. Sprinting to close the gap and catch him, he was about to leap onto another set of tracks. Suddenly out of the corner of his eye he noticed that the string of freight cars that had been waiting on the siding only yards to his left was moving toward him. Knowing he would never make it across, he jumped back to avoid being run over. Then, with a loud squeal of brakes, the freight train stopped, blocking his path to Barlow. By the time Cole had raced around the end of the last car, Barlow had vanished.

Frustrated and angry, Cole Yeager started to search the

yard. Suddenly cannons began booming and church and fire-house bells tolled. Those signals announced the approach of the funeral train, so Cole abandoned his hunt and returned to the station platform feeling disgusted with himself.

Throughout the morning the station platform had buzzed with excited chatter, but once the bells began to ring and the slowly approaching speck grew larger and resolved itself into the shape of a locomotive all conversation ceased. In an awe-struck silence thousands stood in the rain watching the black-draped train inch into the station.

Cole had just stepped onto the platform when he saw the engineer lean out of the cab and look toward the rear of the train. Curious, Cole turned to see the brakeman's hand drop, signaling the engineer to apply the brake so that the car bearing Abraham Lincoln would be aligned with the mark the funeral commission had painted on the bricks of the platform. With a squeal of brakes, the train stopped in a cloud of vented steam.

For one moment everyone stood still. Then the measured tramp of marching feet broke the stillness. The crowd of mourners turned and saw a group of uniformed men known as the Veteran Corps Sergeants moving from the street toward the train, and the throng parted to allow the men onto the platform. At the door to the funeral car the group halted crisply and reshaped their formation into a two-line honor guard while six of their number boarded the car. A moment later the six reappeared bearing Abraham Lincoln's black and silver coffin. Their feet tapping in a reverential cadence, the six pallbearers carried the coffin to the street and then placed it inside the waiting hearse.

That very morning the Baltimore newspapers had described the vehicle as "the most beautiful hearse ever constructed." Its frame was made of rosewood that had been gilded, and the back and sides were of three-quarter-inch-thick plate glass. The newspaper also pointed out that the coffin was resting on patented springs, allowing the body to ride as "gently as if it were on a cloud, with not one annoying jolt."

The hearse rolled away toward the Merchants' Exchange, where the coffin would be opened to allow the thousands of mourners to look upon the President's face. Since the train was scheduled to stay in Baltimore for only four hours, most of the people on the platform followed the hearse, evidently hoping to catch a glimpse of the President.

Moving with the dispersing crowd. Cole went to stand near the locomotive's cowcatcher, the meeting place he had arranged with Matthew Faraday the day before. He had to wait only a few minutes before Faraday and Tamara appeared. Then the threesome found a quiet spot in one of the cars where they could talk privately.

In the welcome warmth and dryness of the car, Cole told them of seeing General Barlow, not only here in Baltimore but in front of Ford's Theater in Washington. "I know it was him," Cole went on. "What I can't understand is why he would deny it. And then to run away like that...I must say, I found his behavior rather odd."

Faraday shrugged and narrowed his blue eyes thoughtfully. "It could be he feels that the atmosphere is such that it would be dangerous for him to admit who he is," he suggested. "Even though he's not one of the conspirators being sought and his name has not been mentioned in connection with the assassination, he might feel that it's best not to let anyone know he was a Rebel general." He stroked his chin for a moment and studied Cole. "Or..." he added, then paused.

"Or?"

"Or he's involved in some activity that he doesn't want

anyone to know about. It's just possible, you know, that he was the one my informant overheard."

Punching his fist into his palm, Cole said, "I should have tried harder to catch him. Perhaps if I hadn't identified myself..."

"Don't be so hard on yourself," Faraday said with a smile. "There's no damage done yet. The body is still safe." Then he paused in thoughtful silence and stared over Cole's shoulder at some unseen idea. "I'll tell you what," he said finally, shifting his gaze back to Cole, "We're going to be changing engines and lines here. The Northern Central is taking over, and our next stop is Harrisburg. Come with me. I'm going to get you on the next freight train going that way."

"There's a passenger train leaving in one hour," Cole pointed out.

"No," Faraday said, shaking his head. "I want you on a freight. It's slow enough to let you have a good, close look at the countryside, and you won't have to worry about passengers or conductors getting in your way."

"All right," Cole agreed. "Whatever you say is fine with me. You're sure you can get me on a freight?"

"Oh, I'm sure I can," Faraday said, smiling. "In the meantime, I'm going to check with a few of my sources back in Washington and see just what I can find out about our mysterious General Barlow."

Five miles northwest of Baltimore, Colonel Manley Daniels and his three men walked their horses through the woods toward a small shack sitting in an open area on the edge of the ballast that lined the track bed. The eight-by-eight-foot unpainted wood building had a small tin smokestack poking through its roof. The windows on the side and back walls were curtained, and while Daniels could not see them, he knew there were a window and a door on the wall that faced the tracks.

Beyond the shack through the steady rain they could see the tracks split, one pair of glistening wet rails going toward Harrisburg and the other set angling sharply away toward Westminster. A switch sent the trains in the right direction. A switchman stayed in the little shack with his set of orders and came out to pull the switch to send each train that came by in the correct direction.

"Colonel, you reckon there's anybody in that shack?" Alan Tatterwall asked softly as they halted their horses at the edge of the woods several yards behind the building. The curtain on the window facing them was closed.

"I'm sure there is," Daniels replied, then he smiled evilly. "But I'll just check on that. You men stay here and tie up these horses."

Daniels dismounted and handed his horse's reins to Tatterwall. He made his way quietly across the grassy area, picked his way over the rocky ballast, and pushed open the door of the shack.

The grizzled, lean switchman who was on duty looked around in surprise. "Who are you?" he asked, pulling his pipe from between his teeth. "What are you doing in here?"

Daniels took off his hat and poured the rainwater from the brim. "I've got a couple of friends with me," he explained, gesturing with his thumb. "We're just looking for a place to get in out of the rain."

"Well, I'm sorry, but you can't come in here," the switchman replied. "This here shack's the property of the Northern Central Railroad, and they don't allow nobody but employees inside."

"The funeral train's coming this way, isn't it?" Daniels asked somberly.

"Yes."

Daniels's hooded dark eyes appealed to the man. "Then have a heart, mister, and let us in."

The switchman studied his visitor for a long moment, his eyes running over the dripping oilskin and muddied boots. Then he shoved back his cap, ran his hand through his graying hair, and sighed. "I see what you're wantin' to do. You're wantin' to pay your respects, aren't you?"

"Yes," Daniels replied. "Yes, that's it. We want to pay our respects."

Screwing up his face in thought, the switchman drummed his fingers on the little wooden shelf that served as his desk. "I reckon that would be all right," he finally said. "Seein' as how we're sort of all in the same boat, so to speak. Sure, tell your friends to come on in. We'll salute together as the train goes by."

"Thank you," Daniels murmured, his voice oozing sincerity. He turned as if to go out the door, but with his hand hidden to the switchman he reached under his oilskin to pull out his pistol. Spinning around, he pointed it toward the railroad man.

"What are you doing?" the switchman yelled in fright.

"I'm paying my respects," Daniels snarled, pulling the trigger. The shot exploding inside the tiny building was so loud that his ears began to ring. A great puff of acrid smoke billowed from the barrel and filled the shack, burning his eyes and nostrils.

The switchman slammed against the wall, his fingers clutching his chest, then he slowly slid to the floor. His eyes were still open, but they had already begun to glaze over with death.

Within a moment Daniels's men were pushing into the shack with their guns drawn, babbling questions about what had happened. Gesturing to the sprawled body through the cloud of gun smoke, the colonel ordered, "Get rid of him before Barlow gets here. There's no need for him to know about this."

"Yes, sir," the three men replied in unison. Picking up the switchman's body, they carried it outside, hauled it some thirty feet down the track, and rolled it down an embankment into some weeds. The thick brush covered the body so well that even though they knew it was there they could not see it.

The body had just nestled into the weeds when they noticed three riders coming toward them.

"We better get out of sight," Lee Hawkins said in a hoarse, nervous voice. He started toward the embankment to hide in the brush.

Alan Tatterwall squinted into the distance. "No, don't worry, it's the general, and that's Dorsey Evans and Buford Posey with him," he said, putting a restraining hand on Hawkins's rain-soaked arm. Pete Chambers nodded in agreement, and the three men started to walk back toward the shack.

Barlow called a greeting when he saw the trio and guided his horse to the shack. Evans and Posey, who was leading a riderless horse, walked their animals a few paces behind him. He dismounted, handed his reins to Evans, and went inside. When he found Daniels alone, he was surprised. "Where's the switchman?" he asked with a frown.

"There was no one here when we arrived," Daniels replied, shrugging.

"No one here? Today, of all days? Don't you think that's a little odd?"

"Yes, sir, I do," Daniels answered, his face filled with wonder.

Barlow sniffed the air.

"You smell gunpowder?" Daniels asked. When Barlow

nodded, Daniels smiled. "I don't wonder. The place was locked, and I had to shoot the lock off to get inside."

"I hope no one heard the shot," Barlow said, clearly worried. Shaking his head, he went to the door. Outside he saw that Tatterwall, Chambers, and Hawkins had walked back and were standing next to Evans and Posey. With a sigh Barlow looked up the spur line, taking in the woods that bordered the track. Then he turned and glanced down the mainline toward Baltimore. "We need to get started!" he announced. "Now, here's what we're going to do." Daniels moved to stand beside him. "I want one man to stay here in the switching house until after the pilot train has passed. Do you have that? Let the pilot engine go by."

"Chambers, that'll be you," Daniels ordered. "You stay here."

"Yes, sir," Pete Chambers promised.

"After the pilot engine has passed," Barlow continued, "throw the switch. That will send the funeral train down the spur line."

"Won't the engineer stop when he sees what's happening?" Tatterwall asked.

"Yes, I'm sure he will," Barlow said. "But you don't stop a train the way you stop a horse. By the time he figures out what's happened and stops the train, the engine and all nine cars will be on the spur. He won't have time to think about putting the engine in reverse before we get on board and make the abduction."

"General, how're we gonna carry that coffin? We got no wagon," Dorsey pointed out.

"We aren't going to carry the coffin," Barlow said, his blue eyes smiling, "We're going to take Lincoln's body out of it, put it in a burlap bag, and throw it over the back of that spare horse we brought."

"General, I hear a train coming," Dorsey cautioned. "You reckon that's the pilot train?"

"No," Barlow said. "It's not time for that yet. But we'd better take these horses into the woods along the spur line and get ready. We don't want anyone on that train to spot us and maybe get suspicious. Dorsey, you take Chambers' horse. Chambers, you know what to do?"

"Yes, sir," Chambers answered.

"Then let's go," Barlow commanded.

CHAPTER SEVEN

COLE YEAGER STOOD IN THE OPEN DOOR OF A BOXCAR looking out as the slow-moving freight train left Baltimore. Despite the steady rain, a large crowd was assembled along the tracks waiting for the funeral train. Only when the train reached the edge of the city did the crowds begin to dwindle until finally the tracksides were deserted. But as the freight passed through each junction, Cole noticed that the switchman would appear in the doorway of his switching house and wave.

Then, about five miles beyond the city limit, the freight train passed a switching house where no one came out. Cole leaned out of the car and looked back as the train rolled by, wondering why this switchman had not appeared. As he stared at the little building, something else "registered on the clean slate of his mind."

There was no smoke. Every other switching house had had a wisp of smoke curling out of its chimney, and as he rode by a couple of them, he could even smell coffee being brewed. This one, however, was cold and quiet. Something was wrong.

Drawing a deep breath, Cole jumped from the slow-moving train and scrambled down the rocky berm. He had timed his leap so he would fall some distance from the shack and tumble into the woods. He wanted to approach it unobserved. The ground was wet and slippery, and he slid all the way down a brushy embankment before coming to a stop. He was startled to discover he had almost fallen into a small ditch filled with flowing mud-brown water. He had not seen the stream because it was hidden in the deep, brushy growth on the edge of the woods. Cole stood up, brushed his clothes off, and decided to follow the stream until he was closer to the shack. It's better to be muddy, he thought, than to approach the building standing straight up in the open...especially if things aren't as they should be.

Cole discovered that they were not as soon as he had taken five steps, because he stumbled and almost fell on a man's body that was lying face down in the muddy stream.

As Cole pushed aside the brush and knelt beside him to take a good look, he thought, *perhaps the man had fallen...perhaps he was a down-on-his-luck derelict who had tried to steal a ride on a freight train.* A quick examination of the body, however, dispelled that thought. This man was wearing good clothes and serviceable shoes. Cole even saw a gold watch chain dangling from his pants pocket. No vagrant would own such luxuries.

Then Cole rolled the man over onto his back and saw a bullet hole in his chest. He touched the man's throat and found it was warm. An icy chill ran up his spine. Instantly he knew who this was and what had happened. This was the switchman, and whoever had killed him was probably hiding in the shack, waiting to use it for some devious purpose. That was why the shack appeared deserted.

Pulling his pistol, Cole made his way toward the

switching house. A curtain hung over the window that faced Cole. He could not see inside, but that also meant that whoever was inside could not see out—at least not through this window.

The last fifty feet of Cole's approach was across open ground. He bent down and moved as stealthily as he could. He was about halfway to the shack when he was suddenly challenged by someone about thirty yards up the spur line that ran toward Westminster from the main track.

"Who the hell are you?" the voice asked sharply.

Thinking the man was a trackwalker who might become innocently involved, Cole signaled for him to be quiet. Desperately, he pointed toward the switching shack, hoping to indicate that the man was placing himself in danger. He then motioned for the man to get down and out of the way.

"Chambers!" the man shouted. "Look, out, Chambers, you got someone sneaking up on you!" Even as the man yelled his warning he was reaching under his oilskin and pulling his pistol.

Suddenly a shot rang out from the shack, and a pistol ball hit the rocks right in front of Cole's feet, then ricocheted behind him. At the same instant, the man Cole had mistaken for a trackwalker also fired.

Cole dived to the ground, falling painfully onto the sharp-edged ballast covering the side of the embankment. Remembering from his battlefield experience always to be a moving target, the agent rolled to his left, scrambling quickly down the berm toward the cover of the brush and the muddy stream at the bottom. As he crawled into the weeds he heard more bullets whistling through the air just above him.

Once in the ditch, Cole turned toward his attackers and returned their fire. By now the man who had shouted the warning had run across the track and was looking down into the ditch, trying to find Cole. Cole shot at him and missed. But his bullet must have come close, because the man darted back to the other side of the track, out of the line of fire. Cole sent a second shot toward the switching house and saw his bullet crash into the window and rip through the curtain.

"Chambers! Come on, let's get out of here!" Cole heard the other man yell.

Cole could not see the door to the shack, but suddenly he spotted a man dashing from the building. Cole shot at him and saw his hat fly from his head. But before he could squeeze off a second round, the man reached the other side of the track and scurried into the brush. Cole scrambled up the embankment and hurried to the track, but both men had vanished. He stood on the rails for a moment, then, realizing that he was making himself a clear target, ran across the track toward the woods in search of the men.

The smell of discharged gunpowder hung in the heavy, wet air, but that was the only sign of the two men with whom he had just done battle. And though he listened carefully, he heard only the splash of rain. With a sigh, he turned to start back up the track when he saw Chambers' hat. Through the crown was a rather large hole that his bullet had made. Had his shot been two inches lower, Cole mused, Chambers would have been lying here dead. He bent to pick up the hat, examined the inside, and found a label that told him the hat came from a shop in Richmond, Virginia. There were no other identifying features. But the fact that the hat had been bought in the capital of the Confederacy was enough to convince Cole that Chambers and his friend belonged to the group he was chasing. Was General Barlow the leader of that group?

He felt a little disgusted with himself. He had practically had them in his hands, and he had let them get away. On the other hand, he had the satisfaction of knowing that he had probably spoiled whatever plan they had hatched—at least for the moment.

Cole dragged the switchman's body back up to the switching shack and left him there so he would be found. He felt a little guilty about just leaving him, but he knew there was nothing more he could do for the poor fellow. It was important that he go on ahead to Harrisburg. He would have to flag the passenger train he had mentioned to Matthew Faraday. Once in the Pennsylvania capital he would wait for the funeral train to arrive and give the detective his report.

When the first shots rang out, the men who were waiting in the woods with General Barlow mounted their nervous animals and held them in check until Pete Chambers and Allan Tatterwall came crashing through the brush. Once they had swung into their saddles, Barlow waved his arm and urged his mount to a gallop. Finding a trail through the woods, the men rode hard for several miles before Barlow decided they were not being pursued. Raising his arm once more, he signaled the men to pull their exhausted horses to a halt in a clearing.

"No, General, he wasn't in any kind of uniform," Alan Tatterwall reported to Earl Barlow when they had, all dismounted and drunk deeply from their canteens.

"Then it wasn't the army or a policeman," Daniels concluded. "I think it was just someone who accidentally came across what we were doing."

"But why was he there?" Barlow asked.

"Maybe it was the relief switchman, just coming to work," Daniels suggested. He flashed a warning look at the three men, who knew that the switchman was dead, to indicate that the murder would remain their secret.

"I could accept that," Barlow mused, looking perplexed, "except that this man was armed. It isn't normal for a switchman to be carrying a weapon of any sort." He turned to Tatterwall, his gaze piercing. "Tell me, was he a big man? Someone well over six feet tall?"

"Yes, sir, he was," Tatterwail answered, surprise in his voice. "I expect he was six feet four or better. How did you know that?"

"Yeager," Barlow declared.

"Yeager?" exclaimed Dorsey Evans. "You mean the man who recognized you at the depot?"

"Yes," Barlow replied. Then he noticed that Daniels was staring at him. "I didn't mention it to you," the general began to explain, "because I thought it was just a coincidence, but I ran into him at the Baltimore station. As a matter of fact, he came up to me and called me by name. But I'm afraid I handled it rather badly. I denied who I was and left quickly. He followed me for a time, but I lost him."

Daniels looked thoughtful for a long moment, then asked, "So what if it was him, General? He doesn't know anything about what we're doing."

"I'm not so sure," Barlow replied slowly. "Perhaps the government has somehow discovered what we plan to do, and Colonel Yeager has been put in charge of stopping us. You know, don't you, that he was an intelligence officer working with Grant? It's not impossible."

"You aren't thinking of calling it off, are you, General?" Daniels demanded, his voice rising.

"I don't know." Barlow shook his head wearily, and his handsome face was haggard. "I'm beginning to doubt that the operation will be successful now. If Colonel Yeager is suspicious, it'll make our task that much more dangerous. I don't know that I have the right to ask you men to take such a risk...especially now that the war is over."

"General," Dorsey Evans put in, "we ain't never backed out on you before, and we ain't fixin' to do it now."

"We're all volunteers, General," Daniels added. "We knew it would be dangerous when we agreed to do it."

Barlow had expected that kind of response from Dorsey, but he was surprised and touched by Daniels's show of support. "Gentlemen, thank you, and you have my assurance that I'll do my best."

All the men were silent for a few moments, then Daniels asked, "Are we going to Harrisburg?"

Barlow stroked his chin in thought. "No," he finally said. "No, I don't think so. The stop after Harrisburg is Philadelphia, and the train won't get there until tomorrow. Let's go there. That will give us a little time to look things over before we make our move."

"Philadelphia," Dorsey murmured. "I've always had a hankerin' to see that place." His face brightened. "Guess I'll finally be gettin' my chance."

When the funeral train pulled into Harrisburg, Pennsylvania, at a little past eight o'clock that evening, a violent rainstorm was in progress. Jagged streaks of lightning flashed across the dark sky while claps of thunder joined the boom of cannons and the tolling of church bells that announced the train's arrival.

The printed schedule told the train's distinguished passengers that Lincoln's body would be removed from the train and taken to the chamber of the state House of Representatives, where it would be displayed. Thousands of mourners would be able to file past the open coffin until midnight, when the chamber would be closed. At eight in the morning, it would be reopened to allow more visitors to view the body for another three hours. Then the casket would be loaded onto the train, and it would travel to Philadelphia.

Matthew Faraday and Tamara Goodnight did not go to the state house with the cortege but remained on the depot platform to meet with Cole. As they stood at the engine's cowcatcher waiting for him, they commented to each other on the large throng at the depot.

Many of the townspeople who did not want to get caught in the crush of the viewing line at the House of Representatives contented themselves with coming down to the big brick station to stare at the train, as if it had taken on some of the Lincoln aura. The train's wet cars gleamed under the new "chemical" lighting system, recently installed at the station, which made the gaslights considerably brighter than before. It was almost as bright as day. Soldiers stood guard at the front and rear of each car to prevent anyone from coming on board. But Tamara had to smile at the children who risked the guards' displeasure by walking all the way up the steps and leaning over to glimpse into the mysterious interior.

About ten minutes after Lincoln's body had been ceremoniously taken away Cole Yeager joined them. Going to a quiet corner inside the depot, the trio sat down and Cole told them what had transpired.

"Well, Cole, you are to be congratulated," Matthew Faraday said after listening to his story. "There is no doubt in my mind that your prompt action today fouled an abduction attempt."

"I'm just sorry I had to leave that switchman's body there," Cole said sadly.

"It couldn't be helped," Faraday replied quickly, seeing that his new agent was troubled. "But I learned over the telegraph that he has been found and by now returned to his family. Tomorrow's papers will no doubt carry the story under the title, 'A Mystery.' The authorities have no idea who shot him or why, and I'm sure they've made no connection whatever to a possible plot to steal the President's body. And I'm afraid we must keep it that way."

"Yes, well, I'm afraid we don't know much more than the authorities, other than the name of one of the men is Chambers," Cole said. "And I don't know who the other one is."

"Nor do I." Faraday smiled and pulled a telegram from his pocket. "But I do know about some of the men involved."

"What? How?"

"Thanks to you, actually, because you recognized General Barlow. I telegraphed Washington, and this message reached me this afternoon." Faraday unfolded the paper and read aloud, "'General Earl Barlow and his chief of staff, Colonel Manley Daniels, reportedly deserted just before Lee's surrender at Appomattox. Some of the officers who served with Barlow believe that he was planning to capture Abraham Lincoln and hold him prisoner until the South was granted favorable terms. This action was not sanctioned by anyone formally representing the Confederate States. The only other person positively identified as being with Barlow and Daniels is a sergeant named Dorsey Evans. The War Department does not believe they were involved in the assassination of the President nor the attack on Secretary Seward. We do not consider Barlow a threat, and we have no further interest in him.'" Faraday folded the telegram, put it back in his pocket, and smiled broadly at Cole. "And now you have identified a fourth man, someone named Chambers. Yes, sir, I would say that, thanks to you, we've made some excellent progress."

Leaning back in his chair, Cole pursed his lips. At that precise moment, the building shook with the boom of a very close thunderclap, and Cole let the rumble die away completely before he spoke. "Thank you for your expression of confidence, Mr. Faraday," Cole said. "But..." he stopped.

"What is it, Cole?"

"I've dealt with General Barlow before, and I found him to be an honorable man."

"You don't believe he could be involved in this?"

Cole sighed and shook his head slowly. "I don't know. If the switchman hadn't been murdered, I might have believed it. General Barlow was a dedicated Confederate, yes, and a ferocious enemy who could, and did, inflict many casualties against us during the war. He might have captured the switchman and held him prisoner until after he had completed his operation, but I find it very hard to believe he would murder him."

"Maybe he had no choice," Tamara suggested. "Maybe the switchman fought back."

"With what?" Cole asked. "He wouldn't have been armed, and Barlow would have known that...if he was involved."

"And you don't think he was?" asked Faraday.

"Well, I know he wasn't one of the two men I saw at the switchman's shack. And Chambers wasn't one of the names in your report. It is possible, isn't it, that whoever is in charge of this plot could be someone other than General Barlow?"

"Yes, of course it's possible," Faraday said, but his voice was skeptical.

"But you don't think so?"

"No. I believe Barlow came to Washington to capture Lincoln, and when Lincoln was assassinated unexpectedly Barlow changed his plans from capturing a live Lincoln to stealing his remains."

Cole shrugged. "Then I guess the best thing for me to do is keep my eyes open for him. If I see Barlow again, then we'll know for certain that he's involved. And if I don't see him..." Cole paused. Then he looked at Faraday, smiled in resignation, and went on, "He might still be involved."

The silver-haired man returned his smile. "Now, Cole, you're beginning to think like a detective."

That evening Cole and Tamara walked to a cafe a few blocks from the depot to have a quiet supper. The meal was simple fare, but it did not matter. Having some time alone to talk did. The violent thunderstorm had passed, leaving behind a windy night with clouds scudding across a crescent moon. It was after ten o'clock when they returned to the funeral train. Matthew Faraday suggested that Cole sleep for a few hours and then leave for Philadelphia during the night. After whispering a tender good night to Tamara, Cole curled his long frame on a bench in the depot and fell off to sleep immediately.

With a smile on her lips Tamara glanced at Faraday and found him grinning at her. She slipped away and returned to her seat on the train. Settling himself on the bench adjacent to Cole's, Matthew Faraday picked up a newspaper, read it, and dozed for a few hours. At 3 A.M. he awoke his new agent and saw him off on a slow-moving freight train bound for Philadelphia. Then he returned to his berth and slept until dawn.

The next morning Tamara noticed that the locomotive on the funeral train was being replaced once more, this time by one belonging to the Pennsylvania Railroad. The new engine was just as beautiful as the previous ones and also draped in black crepe and bedecked with flags. Like the others, it was driven by a proud engineer who considered piloting the funeral train to be the greatest honor of his life.

The train left Harrisburg at a quarter past eleven. The rain that had plagued them for two days was at last over, and as they rolled through towns and cities, Tamara saw that thousands of people were drawn to the trackside, even though the train would not be stopping. At one point she saw a big sign which read: ABRAHAM LINCOLN, THE ILLUS-TRIOUS MARTYR OF LIBERTY, THE NATION MOURNS HIS LOSS. THOUGH DEAD, HE STILL LIVES.

At Lancaster, Faraday pointed to an old man who was sitting in a buggy at the depot, his hat held respectfully in his hands as the train rolled without stopping through the station.

"Do you recognize him?" he asked.

Tamara gasped. "That's...that's former President Buchanan, isn't it?"

"Yes."

As the train continued on its journey, Tamara was struck with scenes that she knew would stay in her memory for the rest of her life. Shops and factories were closed, and the population of every town and village along the way was turned out beside the tracks to stand in silence or, in many cases, to kneel. Once she spotted a solitary farmer at work behind his plow on a far, lonely hill. As the train neared, the distant figure knelt and bowed his head.

The closer the train got to Philadelphia, the larger the crowds. It was still several miles from the city limits when Tamara realized there were no gaps at all along the tracks, just solid lines of people. When the train finally arrived at the Broad Street Station at half past four, more people were waiting at the depot than Tamara had ever seen at one time in her life.

Many of the train's passengers got off to mingle with the crowd, but since Faraday and Tamara had a particularly good view of the proceedings through the window at their seats, they stayed on board to watch.

It took longer to get the coffin off the train in Philadelphia than it had anywhere else, due in part to the size of the crowd.

With great pomp and ceremony, the honor guard loaded the coffin onto the waiting hearse, which was draped in black and white and crowned with three enormous white plumes that waved at the top of the canopy. Eight black horses, their coats gleaming in the sun, pulled Lincoln's body toward Independence Square. Booming cannons and tolling bells announced the departure of the hearse from the station. Accompanying the hearse were eleven marching units playing slow dirges and tapping muffled drums.

Rising from his seat, Faraday left Tamara on board and disembarked from the train. He went directly to the depot's telegraph office where he expected to find a message from Cole Yeager. Instead of a message, however, he saw a very tall man leaning against the wall with his arms folded across his chest.

Faraday smiled as he approached him. "You know, Cole, you will have one problem in this business," he observed.

"What's that?"

"It's practically impossible for you to blend in," he said with a chuckle. "I spotted you from the front door."

Cole laughed. "Well, there are two sides to the picture. It is hard for me to blend in, but if I want to be found, I have the advantage."

"True, true," Faraday replied, his blue eyes amused. Then he grew serious. "Have you seen Barlow anywhere?"

Cole shook his head. "No. I've looked all over the city, but I haven't seen him. Of course, a policeman told me that about three hundred thousand people have congregated here to mourn for Lincoln. In a crowd that large he would be hard to spot. He could be anywhere."

"Yes," Faraday agreed. "But if he is the one behind the plot to steal the body, that means he'll have to be where it is...at least once."

"I understand that Mr. Lincoln's body will be on view in the east wing of Independence Hall," Cole said.

"Then that's where we'll go." The detective turned to walk toward the door that led to the street. He had taken a few steps when he realized that Cole had not moved. Glancing back at the young man, he saw him looking through the crowd that was still milling around the station.

"Where is Tamara?" Cole asked, a puzzled frown on his face.

"She's still on the train," Faraday said, stepping back to stand beside him. "As a matter of fact, I think it would be good for her to stay on board—just in case our friends decide to sneak onto the train and try something while everyone's attention is diverted."

A worried frown creased Cole's forehead. "You...you don't think she's in danger, do you?"

Faraday laughed easily and put his hand on Cole's arm. "My friend, she strikes me as being a very resourceful young woman. If she senses any danger, I'm certain she'll know what to do."

Cole laughed sheepishly. "I guess you're right. I sounded like a possessive brother, didn't I?"

"I wouldn't exactly say your interest sounded brotherly," the detective replied wryly. "And I don't think Tamara would think of it that way, either."

Cole sighed. "Is it that obvious?"

"Only a little less than if you were to wear a sign around your neck," Faraday teased.

At that same moment in another part of town, across the street from Independence Square, General Earl Barlow and his men watched the funeral parade, On the front of the Old State House there was a large transparency of Lincoln, lighted by brilliant gas lamps that spelled out the words HE STILL LIVES. The square was illuminated by red, white, and blue calcium lamps, which had the rather incongruous effect of introducing bright colors into a somber sea of mourners.

In order to get a good view of the hearse, people had jammed into the street, barely leaving a path wide enough for the parade to pass. The tops of buildings and roofs of porches were filled with people, and men and boys climbed into trees or clung to telegraph poles.

"You ever seen so many people?" Dorsey Evans asked.

"Not even if everybody I'd ever seen in my life was to suddenly show up at the same time," Buford Posey replied.

Pete Chambers laughed. "Look at the police," he said, pointing to three or four officers who were trying to move the throng back out of the street to let the cortege pass. "There's no way they can handle this crowd."

"That's it!" Barlow exclaimed, striking his fist into his palm. He looked at Chambers and smiled broadly. "You've given me an idea!"

"I did? But I didn't say anything," Chambers said.

"Oh, but you did," Barlow assured him. "Come on, men, we've got to find some place where we can talk."

The members of the Philadelphia funeral commission had realized that they would have a problem filing the large numbers of mourners through the front door of Independence Hall and out again. Assessing their alternatives carefully, they had decided to close the main door of the hall and build scaffolds at each of the two front windows of the east wing. The windows were large and high. The mourners would stand in line behind rope barriers in the street, enter the vast hall through one of the front windows, file past the open coffin on a platform that, ran alongside it, and leave the hall through the second window. A strong balustrade encircling the bier would prevent the mourners from getting too close to the body. The commission members also decided that police should be on hand to hurry the people along. The mourners would not be allowed to stop for even a second before they exited through the second window.

Viewing on the first night was to be by invitation only, and the list consisted mostly of wounded war veterans. This evening's viewing was expected to be quiet and well controlled, with as many policemen on hand as there were visitors. With those safeguards Matthew Faraday and Cole Yeager were certain that nothing untoward would occur.

As they had anticipated, the viewing that first evening was uneventful. But by 5:00 Sunday morning, Faraday and Cole had positioned themselves on the steps of Independence Hall. They planned that Cole, who knew Barlow on sight, would stroll around the building at half-hour intervals and survey the crowd, while Faraday would remain in front of the building, looking for signs of trouble.

By dawn the lines of mourners had stretched as far as the Schuylkill River on the west and to the Delaware River on the east. In addition, the crowds were growing larger by the hour because more people were crossing by ferry from New Jersey. Many of the mourners had been in line all night, but even those who were newly arrived were just as tired because Philadelphia's blue law would not allow the horse-cars to run on Sunday. As a result, the great majority of people had walked several miles to get to the end of a line that promised a seven-hour wait at best.

The crowd was irritable, tired, and keyed-up. Conditions were perfect for Earl Barlow's meticulously prepared plan to succeed. He and his men were huddled against a building a block away from Independence Hall.

Barlow quickly scanned the crowd one last time and turned to his men with a satisfied smile. "All right, men, everything is just right," he said softly. "Move through the crowd toward Independence Hall and start picking pockets."

"Does it matter whose pockets we pick?" Dorsey whispered.

"No. As I said last night, it won't take much to set these people off. If a group of pickpockets starts working them, the crowd will turn into an angry mob very quickly. And when it does..." Barlow let the sentence hang.

"We go to work," Daniels finished it for him. "Precisely!"

"General, is it all right if we just choose the fat, rich-lookin' ones?" Dorsey asked as he scanned the crowd. "It ain't gonna set too well in my craw to be stealin' from the workin' folk."

"That's exactly who I want you to go after— the rich," Barlow assured him, smiling. "They're the ones who squeal the loudest when they lose something."

"That means more money for us," Alan Tatterwall said with a greedy gleam in his murky brown eyes.

Barlow's blue eyes snapped. "We're not doing this for gain," he said sharply.

Scratching his head, Tatterwall asked, "Well, General, you're not suggestin' we give the money back, are you?"

"No. I want you to throw it in the middle of the crowd."

Tatterwall's mouth dropped open. "Excuse me for askin', General, but why the hell would we do a damn fool thing like that?"

"Because it'll just get the crowd that much more stirred up," Daniels replied dryly. "Right, General?"

"That's it."

"I think it's a good idea," Darnels agreed.

"If you say so," Tatterwall said with a shrug. "But if I get my hands on a nice, fat wallet, I'm liable to pull out a few greenbacks for myself before I drop the rest." He turned and started into the throng with Hawkins, Daniels, and Chambers close on his heels. Barlow glared at Tatterwall's back, then shook his head and gestured to Evans and Posey to come with him.

"Look at them," Cole Yeager said quietly to Matthew Faraday. He was nodding at the people standing in lines behind the ropes as they moved slowly in one window and out the other. Cole was just returning from a slow sweep around the exterior of Independence Hall and joining Faraday, who was standing on the front steps. "The poor souls—

many of them have stood patiently for seven or eight hours, waiting for a glimpse that lasts no longer than a second."

"No, you're wrong about that," Faraday said. "It'll last a lifetime. Several lifetimes in fact, for they'll pass on stories to their children and grandchildren of how they were privileged to look into Lincoln's face."

"Hey, watch it!" someone in the crowd shouted angrily.

"Look out here!" another called.

A disturbed murmuring rose from the crowd. It was punctuated by another angry shout, then a general shifting about. People began straining against the rope lines.

"What is it?" Cole asked. "What's going on?"

"I don't know," Faraday admitted. Instantly, his senses were alert, and he started scanning the crowd, trying to find out what was going on.

"Pickpocket!" someone shouted.

"Stop that man!" another called. "Stop that man! He stole my wallet."

"Quit shoving! I've been standing here all night to hold on to this spot!"

"Here's another thief!" someone yelled.

The crowd, which had been moving in an orderly fashion, began to break apart, milling and surging about. Three or four of the many policemen who were positioned outside the building started toward the line.

Suddenly Cole saw Earl Barlow, dressed in the same coat and hat he had been wearing in Baltimore, leaning against one of the retaining ropes holding a knife in his hand. "There's Barlow!" he shouted, pointing toward the man. "What's he about to do?"

Following Cole's outstretched arm, Faraday's sharp blue eyes focused on the man in the gray hat. "He's going to cut the ropes!" he exclaimed, and at that precise moment, the rope went slack. Although the barriers had been psychological rather than physical, when they disappeared so, too, did all sense of restraint. The crowd surged forward as one large mob.

The police, realizing that they suddenly had a riot on their hands, blew their whistles, abandoned their posts, and rushed to try to quell the disturbance. Even those policemen stationed inside the east wing of Independence Hall raced outside to deal with the riot. In their mad rush, however, they only exacerbated the situation. They grabbed the person at the window who was just stepping in to view Lincoln and forced him and everyone in line behind him to go to the rear of the line.

"You can't do this to us!" one of the men shouted. "We've waited all night to get this far!"

Others joined in the protest, but the police, clearly determined to restore peace at any cost, ignored all objections. The shouting, cursing, and shoving intensified.

Suddenly Faraday knew what it was all about. "Come on!" he shouted. "We've got to get to Lincoln! This is a diversion!"

Cole understood immediately what Faraday meant. Faraday broke into a run and began to push his way toward the scaffold at the right-hand window; Cole was beside him. The two men vaulted onto the scaffold, pushed aside several mourners who were trying to leave the chamber, and stepped through the window. They were shocked to see several mourners still in the room. In their rush to deal with the confusion on, the street, the police had neglected to clear the viewing chamber. Cole spun around just in time to see someone trying to climb in through a back window that had been shoved open.

"Hold it, Chambers!" Cole shouted, recognizing the intruder as one of the two men he had exchanged shots with at the switchman's shack.

Chambers had just cleared the sill. Still in an awkward

crouch he whipped out his pistol and fired at Cole. One of the mourners screamed, but the bullet went wild, barreling into the ceiling molding.

As the shot thundered in his ears, Cole heard Faraday shout, "Get down! Everyone, drop to the floor!"

Cole felt rather than saw the handful of men and women scramble for cover. For a brief instant he thought of the innocent people in the room about to be caught in a deadly cross fire, but he knew he had no choice. He pulled out his own weapon and triggered a shot. Chambers was about to fire another round when Cole's bullet slammed into his chest, Chambers' gun went off, the shot deafening, and the ball shattered the plaster high on the wall. Then Chambers fell backward through the window.

Ignoring the screaming woman mourner huddled on the floor, the two agents dashed across the room and peered cautiously out the window. On the ground below they saw Chambers sprawled on his back, a red stain blossoming on his shirtfront. Several other men were running away, heading around the building and toward the crowd in the front. It was impossible to shoot at them without risking injury to innocent bystanders.

Faraday and Cole scrambled out of the window and started to pursue the fleeing men. "Stop those men!" Faraday yelled, but his words went unheeded. The agents scurried as best they could through the milling throng, finding their way blocked with almost every step. But the men they were chasing were having just as hard a time, so they could not widen their lead. Repeatedly, Faraday and Cole found themselves drawing closer to their prey only to have the men elude them.

Then, as the crowd got more and more out of hand, they found the going even harder. What had been a peaceable assembly turned ugly as bonnets were pulled off women's heads, hats were knocked flying, dresses were ripped, and jackets were torn. The square was filled with screams and curses and fighting, all of which served to divert Faraday and Cole, and finally, running out of breath, they lost sight of their quarry and halted. The men they had been pursuing got away.

When they returned to Independence Hall, they found a couple of policemen standing over Chambers' body. It was soon evident that the police thought the man had been killed because he was one of the pickpockets who prompted the riot. Faraday pulled Cole to one side to talk quietly to him.

"This was one of the men you saw?"

"Yes. And the other man I saw was with the fellows who got away."

"And we both saw Barlow cutting the ropes. There's no longer any doubt that he's involved, is there?"

"No doubt whatever," Cole agreed.

Faraday sighed. "I know you don't wish to believe such a thing about a man you considered an honorable adversary, but we deal in evidence, not ideals—and the evidence is that General Barlow is behind this dreadful plot. Are you prepared to deal with him if need be?"

"Yes, of course," Cole assured him. He pointed toward Chambers' body and the policemen gathered around it. "I don't suppose we're going to tell them what really happened, are we?"

"Absolutely not." Faraday shook his head; his craggy face was grim. "If word got out that this was an attempt to steal Lincoln's body, the rest of the funeral train's journey would be canceled. Then the President's body would have to be taken surreptitiously to his grave the way he had to sneak into Washington in the first place. That would be a repudiation of everything Lincoln fought and died for. The war has been won, the country is free, and the people should be allowed to express their grief and show their affection for the man who led them through the long, dark night. Don't you agree?"

"Yes, completely," Cole replied, his face somber.

"Then we'll say nothing."

CHAPTER EIGHT

THE TAMMANY-CONTROLLED CITY COUNCIL IN NEW YORK WAS determined that there would be no repeat of the riot that took place in Philadelphia. In the "City of Brotherly Love" it had taken the police until one o'clock the next morning to restore order. New York would not experience what Philadelphia had. The city fathers were adamant about that.

One way to prevent it, they decided, was to decree that there would be "no black people in the procession." When it was pointed out to them that blacks had had absolutely nothing to do with the riot in Philadelphia, they nevertheless stood by the order to ban Negroes from the funeral procession.

The blacks were indignant over the order. Why would the race Abraham Lincoln had freed be denied the chance to honor him in New York? Even a prestigious periodical rallied to their cause, reminding its readers that the Negro people feel particularly deserted with their best friend gone. No one will miss the President more than they. Yet, despite all the protestation, City Hall was unyielding and would not be swayed.

With all the preparations made, the city then donned funereal bunting and waited as the funeral train made its way slowly through the early-morning darkness from Philadelphia. At dawn, the train stopped at the Trenton station for half an hour—a small concession to the state of New Jersey. It was little enough, the disgruntled lawmakers insisted, since Trenton was the only state capital on the entire route where Lincoln would not be taken from the train for a complete funeral service.

General Townsend agreed to let the train stop. The city fathers quickly organized a commemorative service to be held at the depot. They were determined to fill the half-hour stop with as much pomp and ceremony as possible.

During the brief ceremony, Matthew Faraday checked in at the telegraph office in the Trenton depot. There he found a message from Cole, who had gone ahead to New York City the day before, stating that he had seen no further sign of General Barlow or his men.

Leaving the telegraph office to return to the train, Faraday noticed a Negro soldier in full-dress uniform, a sergeant major from a black infantry regiment, who was standing in his path several feet away. Faraday quickly looked at his uniform and saw that in addition to the rather imposing braid, stripes, and buttons there was a medal pinned to his breast pocket. The detective recognized it as the Medal of Honor.

The man stepped in front of Faraday and, coming to attention, saluted. "Excuse me, suh, but are you Mr. Faraday?"

"I am," he replied with a nod. "Whom do I have the honor of addressing?"

"I am Sergeant Major Uriah McCoy."

"Hello, Sergeant Major," Faraday said, smiling. "I see you've come down to pay your last respects to the President."

Then he looked at the soldier more closely. "Did you say Uriah McCoy?"

"Yes, suh," the black soldier replied.

"Sergeant Major, during the war an agent of mine secured the services of a volunteer to gather some valuable information about the Confederate works around Franklin. As I recall, that volunteer was a Negro soldier who disguised himself as a slave to go behind enemy lines. That hero's name was McCoy. Do I have the honor of addressing that same gentleman?"

"The honor is all mine, suh."

Smiling broadly, Faraday reached out to shake the soldier's hand. "That was a very brave thing you did, Sergeant Major. If you had been caught, the Rebels would have no doubt taken particular delight in hanging you."

"Yes, suh, I 'spect so," McCoy replied, his deep brown eyes twinkling. He touched his medal. "And that's how my commandin' officer, Cap'n Poindexter, come to get this medal for me. I have a letter from him, askin' you if you would be so kind as to allow me to introduce myself." He started to reach inside his pocket, but Faraday stopped him.

"No need to show me the letter, Sergeant Major. I recall Captain Poindexter speaking very highly of you. But I take it you wanted more than just to meet me?"

"Yes, sir," McCoy said. "Mr. Faraday, Cap'n Poindexter says that you're a man of powerful influence with the Secretary of War…that the secretary listens to you. He told me that if there'd be anybody on this here train who could help us with our problem, it'd be you."

"I have been able to get the secretary to listen upon occasion," Faraday admitted wryly. "What exactly is the nature of your problem?"

"I want the secretary to let me and the other colored folk that live in New York walk in the parade that's honorin' the

President," McCoy explained. He quickly told Faraday about the edict that had come down from City Hall. "Somehow, Mr. Faraday, it don't seem right—us gettin' left out like that."

Faraday recalled the touching scene just outside the Washington depot where an entire black regiment had lined up alongside the track to pay their last respects. Though not allowed to come into the depot, this same regiment had marched as a guard of honor in the Washington cortege. He was offended that a great city like New York would bar the very people who had been the focus of so much of Lincoln's attention over the last four years. He studied the sergeant who stood so nobly before him, then sighed and ran his hand through his silvery hair.

"I agree with you, Sergeant Major. It doesn't seem right for you to be left out. I'll send a telegram to the Secretary of War, expressing in the strongest language possible my outrage over this policy. I can't guarantee you that anything will come of it, but I will try."

"Thank you, suh."

A twinkle played in Faraday's eyes. "Tell me, Sergeant Major, how will you return to New York?"

"There's a train leavin' just after the funeral train," McCoy replied.

"How would you like to ride to New York with me, as my guest, on board the funeral train?" McCoy's eyes grew wide, and then tears welled in them. "Do you mean that? You would fix it so's I could ride on the train with Father Abraham?"

"Yes," Faraday told him gently.

"But I'm colored," McCoy protested.

"Yes, I noticed," Faraday said with a wry smile. He held up his finger. "Wait right here while I send the telegram to Washington." Faraday turned, hurried back to the telegraph office, and sent a wire to Stanton, asking him to intervene in the situation in New York City. When he returned a few minutes later, the soldier was waiting for him in exactly the same spot. With Sergeant Major McCoy at his side, Faraday walked to one of the passenger cars. He asked McCoy to wait outside for a few minutes, then stepped onto the funeral train to speak with General Townsend, the senior army officer on board.

Faraday found the general in the dining car where he had escaped the press of mourners; he was having a cup of coffee. Smiling warmly, the detective sat down at his table and said, "General Townsend, there's a soldier here in Trenton who performed a valuable service for me during the war—a service for which, I might add, he was awarded the Medal of Honor."

"What's that? The Medal of Honor, you say?" Townsend asked. The general raised his eyebrows in astonishment.

"Yes, sir."

"And what did you say his name was?"

"McCoy, sir. Sergeant Major McCoy."

"Well, the Irish certainly did perform some valuable services for us during the war. I remember the New York Irish Brigade and how well they fought. I'd like to meet this sergeant major."

"I was hoping for more than that, General," Faraday said. "I would like you to authorize him to ride with us, just as far as New York."

"Just to New York? Why, of course," Townsend agreed airily. "I can't see any problem with that. We'll be in the city before the day is out, and we wouldn't even have to make special arrangements for him. Bring him on board, with my blessing."

"Would you put that in writing, General?" Faraday asked. Noting the general's puzzled expression, he smiled. "Mr.

Ward and some of the others might question it," he explained.

"Certainly. I'd be happy to," Townsend replied, and, when Faraday handed him a piece of paper, the officer put his cup of coffee down and wrote: "Sergeant Major McCoy is granted passage to New York on board the presidential Funeral Train by authority of Brigadier General Edward Townsend, Commanding Officer." Townsend then handed it to Faraday with a flourish, "There. How's that?"

"That's fine. Thank you, General."

"I always like to meet with Medal of Honor winners and with our noncommissioned officers. You know, Napoleon once said that the noncommissioned officer was the back-bone of any army, and I believe he was right. Now, bring your Irishman on board."

Faraday stepped to the door and looked out toward the platform where Sergeant Major McCoy stood waiting, tall and erect. "Sergeant Major McCoy," he called. He held up the paper Townsend had just signed. "Here's your authority. Now, come aboard. General Townsend would like to meet you."

Townsend was smiling broadly until he saw the black face of the sergeant-major whose presence on the train he had just authorized. Then his smile froze, and he looked over at Faraday, whose own smile, by contrast, was very genuine.

"General Townsend, Suh," McCoy said, saluting sharply. "I want to express my thanks to you for lettin' me on this train."

Townsend cleared his throat, then returned McCoy's salute. "Uh, yes," he mumbled. "Well, I'm always glad to do what I can for a winner of the Medal of Honor." He looked over at Faraday. "I thought you said this man was an Irishman."

"No, sir," Faraday replied. "I said he was a Medal of Honor winner. You said he was an Irishman."

"I reckon I'm an Irishman at that, General," Sergeant Major McCoy put in, smiling broadly. "A black Irishman."

General Townsend looked over at Faraday, who was having a hard time controlling his laughter. Finally Townsend relaxed, and a warm, welcoming smile creased his face. He reached out and shook McCoy's hand. "Then black Irishman it is, soldier," he declared. "I'm glad to have you aboard."

By the time the train arrived in New York and the solemn procession began, the initial City Hall orders regarding the presence of blacks had been changed. In explaining the new orders, the City Hall officials quoted a telegram they had received from Secretary of War Stanton:

IT HAS BEEN BROUGHT TO MY ATTENTION THAT NEGROES ARE BEING EXCLUDED FROM THE HONORS THE CITY OF NEW YORK IS PAYING TO OUR MARTYRED PRESIDENT. I FEEL THIS WOULD BE DIRECTLY CONTRARY TO THE WISHES OF PRESIDENT LINCOLN AND IT IS THE DESIRE OF THE SECRETARY OF WAR THAT NO DISCRIMINATION RESPECTING COLOR SHOULD BE EXERCISED IN ADMITTING PERSONS TO THE FUNERAL PROCESSION.

This was the largest parade of all; more than one hundred thousand people took part in a procession that lasted several hours. It was massive, spectacular, and dazzling, yet somber. The last unit in the parade was a delegation of over two thousand blacks, many dressed in Union Army uniforms, and marching proudly at the head of the black delegation was Sergeant Major Uriah McCoy. McCoy was holding one of the posts of a banner which read: TO MILLIONS OF BONDMEN, LIBERTY HE GAVE.

After leaving New York, the train chugged north along the Hudson River toward the state capital at Albany. Great bonfires and torches borne by solemn citizens lighted the entire route. The mourners who had come to watch the train were paying their final respects, and their very numbers prevented General Barlow and his men from making another attempt at stealing the body. General Barlow and his men were riding ahead of the funeral train on horseback, vainly searching for an opportune place to try once again to steal the President's body.

"What are we going to do, General?" Dorsey Evans asked as they made camp on the night of April 25. "There's just solid lines of people no matter where we go. Don't look to me like we're gonna ever get another chance to get him."

Barlow patted his loyal sergeant on the shoulder. "Don't worry, Dorsey, we'll get our chance. Naturally the tracks are all going to be crowded here...this area is densely populated. But soon the train will head west—to places like Ohio, Indiana, and Illinois. There are desolate sections of track in those states that stretch for many miles between very small towns. When we get there, we'll find the opportunity we've been looking for."

"Damned if I don't think it would've been easier to snatch him when he was still alive," Lee Hawkins cried.

"Yeah, if I'd'a known how much trouble that fella Booth, was gonna cause us, I'd'a stopped him myself," Buford Posey said. "You reckon they'll find him. General?"

"I imagine they will," Barlow replied. "He's the most hunted man in the history of this country."

Manley Daniels shook his head. "They'll never catch him," he insisted. "Once he gets to the South, he'll be treated like a hero."

"I hope not," Barlow countered. "I would hate to see such a cowardly act rewarded."

"How can you say that, General?" Daniels wanted to know. "John Wilkes Booth struck a blow for the Confederacy."

"Perhaps. But he struck that blow from the cloak of darkness. I'd hardly say such a cowardly act would bring honor to our cause."

"The Yankees will never find him," Daniels insisted.

But even as Daniels spoke those words, Edwin Stanton's people were closing in on the assassin. Before dawn the next morning, on a farm near Port Royal, Virginia, a detachment of twenty-five soldiers caught up with John Wilkes Booth and shot him dead.

While the rest of the country celebrated the fact that Booth had been killed and his coconspirators caught, the funeral train continued on its sorrowful journey. After leaving Albany, it went on to Buffalo without incident. From there, it headed to Ohio.

At dawn on April 28, two weeks after the assassination, the train reached the outskirts of Cleveland. Here, the city fathers planned to hold the funeral in the park, and an open-sided Chinese pagoda was built for the purpose.

During the funeral parade it rained, but no one seemed to notice. Unlike Philadelphia, where people had to wait on interminably long lines, everyone in Cleveland who wanted to view the body was able to.

The locomotive was changed again in Cleveland. This time it was to the same engine that had brought Lincoln east four years ago. The engineer from that inaugural journey had died, but the fireman on that trip, George Martin, was the proud engineer this time, and the original conductor, E. D. Page, was again serving in that capacity.

It was late at night when the funeral train pulled out of the Cleveland depot and resumed its journey. Tamara Goodnight stared out the window at the darkness, lost in thought.

Somewhere out there, she knew, Cole Yeager was riding through the night and the rain on a desperate, lonely mission to protect the cargo that was so precious to the nation. He was fighting the elements and quite possibly facing extreme danger, all alone. And what made it more difficult, she thought, was that no one would ever know. It's one thing to perform some heroic service for your country and receive your reward, she told herself, but it's quite another to perform a service that will never be rewarded, never even be known.

Upset and concerned for Cole, she had talked to Matthew Faraday about it. "If we are successful," he began, "when historians read about this train of glory a hundred years from now, there won't be the slightest hint that the body was ever in danger. Our knowledge of a job well done will be our only reward, and we will take that to our grave."

"That's reward enough for me," Tamara said. "My role in this has been very small. But Cole is risking his life—"

Faraday interrupted her, "Which will make success an even greater reward for him."

Tamara looked out into the darkness and saw yet another bonfire with several mourners huddling around it. All these people, she thought. How awful it would be if General Barlow and his men had their way and they were denied their right to grieve.

General Barlow and his band of raiders had been traveling just ahead of the train ever since it left New York City, still waiting for another chance to steal the body. Even though Barlow had promised that once the train got out west there would be many opportunities, the truth was they were still frustrated, because even in the most remote areas, the trackside was crowded with mourners. Then, while studying a railroad map of Ohio, Barlow found what he thought might be the ideal spot. About fifty miles north of Columbus, Ohio, a spur line branched off to Marysville. That track left the main line at a point known as North Switch, with the return track rejoining it about a half mile away at South Switch.

Barlow smiled broadly, putting his finger on the map. "All right," he declared, "here's where we're going to do it."

Gathering his men around the small camp fire, he outlined his plan. "We are going to split up. Most of us will go here, to Marysville," he began, pointing to the map. "There, we will steal an engine and bring it to North Switch. Meanwhile, Dorsey, you and Buford will go to South Switch. Now, after the pilot engine passes both North and South Switch and the funeral train passes North Switch, you two will block the track at South Switch so the funeral train can't proceed any farther. The rest of us will bring the stolen engine onto the main track at North Switch and back it up to the funeral car, which is the last car on the train. After hooking the engine up to the funeral car, we'll pull it away from the rest of the train, and once we are far enough away, we'll remove Lincoln's body and leave the car and honor guard stranded. No one will get hurt, and we'll have accomplished our mission." He looked at each of the men, then asked, "Do you have any questions?"

Dorsey nodded. "General, what's to keep the funeral train from just backin' up after us?"

"Good point," Barlow replied. "All right, we'll disable the train in some way...perhaps derail one of the cars before we leave."

"There's another problem," Daniels pointed out.

"What's that?"

"The honor guard."

Barlow chuckled. "An old general and an overweight admiral, neither of whom is armed. I don't think they'll be much of a problem at all, Colonel."

"They both have eyes," Daniels remarked. "They can give the authorities information on us."

"That's just a chance we'll have to take," Barlow replied. "No operation is risk-free."

"We can improve our chances by killing the Honor Guard," Daniels suggested.

Barlow flashed an angry glance at the officer. "Colonel Daniels, I didn't hear that comment."

"I was just giving you all the options. General, as a good second-in-command should."

"Yes, well, killing innocent people is no option." Barlow folded up his map. "Now, let's get this fire out. We have lots of work to do. We have to steal an engine before the funeral train gets here."

It was after three o'clock in the morning when Cole Yeager rode into the whistle-stop town of Cardington, Ohio. Bonfires and torches burned along the tracks, and the gas lamps at the depot were ablaze. Although it was two hours before the Lincoln train was due to pass through, and even though it was not scheduled to stop, several hundred mourners had already gathered at the tracks.

Cole looked at all the people who were standing in the glow waiting for the train. There were very old people and very young children, prosperous businessmen and poor farmers, beautiful young ladies and women whose clothes and features bore the mark of years of hard work. There were soldiers and ex-soldiers, some in fresh elegant looking uniforms and some in uniforms that were little more than tattered rags, evidence of years of hard campaigning. Some of the soldiers had empty sleeves and trouser legs, having left a limb at such places as Shiloh, Gettysburg, and the Wilderness. But here in the flickering light of torches and bonfires, all were joined by their common sorrow over Lincoln's death.

The agent dismounted, tied his horse to a rail behind the depot, and went inside the building. He was surprised to see that the lunch counter was open. It would normally be closed at this hour, but the enterprising proprietor had apparently decided to take advantage of the crowd. However, it appeared that very few people were willing to pay five cents for a cup of coffee or to buy a sandwich. Except for two patrons, the counter was empty. The proprietor was obviously disappointed by his lack of business, because when Cole stepped up to buy a cup of coffee, he seemed to find it an imposition and served it listlessly.

Cole looked at the other two customers and saw from their uniforms that one was the stationmaster and the other was the telegrapher. They were sitting at the end, talking together. Picking up his cup and moving down the counter to join them, Cole said to the telegrapher, "Excuse me, sir. My name is Cole Yeager. Do you have any messages for me?"

"Yeager? Yeager? No, I don't think so," he replied. "Why? Should I?"

"Not necessarily," Cole said. "But I'm traveling ahead of my employer, and he often wires instructions ahead to me at the next stop."

"Well, I've received nothing."

The stationmaster pulled out his watch and looked at it. "One hour and forty-five minutes before the train comes through," he announced.

"Maybe when the officials on the train see so many people waiting here they'll stop," the telegrapher said.

"No, no, they are on a very strict schedule."

"Listen," Cole said, interrupting their discussion, "has a group of riders come through here recently—people who might have caught your interest because of the way they were acting?"

"Are you kidding, mister? Look at the people out there!"

147

The stationmaster turned in his seat and pointed toward the window.

"Yes, I've seen them," Cole replied, trying to keep the impatience out of his voice. "But there's nothing suspicious about any of those people. They're obviously here to see the funeral train."

The stationmaster shrugged. "They're the only people I've seen."

Cole moved closer to them and dropped his voice. "Look, it's very important I find these men. You've seen no one doing anything that seemed out of the ordinary?"

"Mister, this entire night is filled with people doing something that's out of the ordinary," the stationmaster snapped in exasperation. "Do you think it's normal for hundreds of people to be standing alongside the railroad track at three o'clock in the morning?"

"I guess not," Cole admitted. He was desperate for information, any thread or hint that might give him a clue to where Barlow and his men were. But he did not know what to ask, and his questions sounded pointless even to him. He drummed his fingers on the counter, frustrated by his lack of success at finding out anything.

Then the telegrapher chuckled. "That's not the only thing out of the ordinary," he said and then turned to the stationmaster. "You mind that message we got a couple of hours ago?"

"What message?" Cole asked.

The telegrapher chuckled again; "It don't make much sense, but it seems that over to Marysville, someone stole a locomotive and tender late last night. That seems a little out of the ordinary, wouldn't you say?"

"What? An engine and tender?" Cole exclaimed. "Have they found it yet? Do they know who took it?"

The stationmaster laughed. "Well, now, that don't much

matter, does it? I mean, there ain't nowhere them fellas can go with it, 'cept stay on the track. It's kind of a dumb thing to do, if you ask me."

"Them fellas? You mean there was more than one?"

"Quite a little group of them, from the way the message read. Probably some veterans out for a good time. The stationmaster over in Marysville thought they might be soldiers—leastwise, they acted like soldiers."

"Barlow," Cole muttered, shaking his head.

The stationmaster stared at the agent. "Who's this Barlow, fella?" he asked. "Look here, do you think you know who it was that did such a fool thing?"

"Yeah," Cole replied. "I think I know. You have a map?"

"Over there, on the wall, there's a big one of the whole state of Ohio. Every railroad is clearly marked."

Hurrying across the room, Cole studied the map. He quickly located Marysville, then North and South Switch, all a few miles south of Cardington. He put one finger on North Switch and another on South Switch, then let out a long, slow sigh. "Damn," he breathed. "I don't know exactly what you have in mind, Barlow, but I sure as hell know where you're planning to do it."

"Did you say somethin', Mister?" the station- master called, hearing Cole mumble.

"No," Cole answered, still studying the map.

The railroad man then suggested, "If you're plannin' to watch the funeral train come through, you'd better get out there and find yourself a place to stand. Folks are still comin' from all around, and pretty soon all the good places will be taken."

The telegraph instrument suddenly started clacking, and the telegrapher went over to read it. Thinking it might be a message for him. Cole waited, but the telegrapher looked at the station- master;

"It's Marcus Pell over in Marion. He wants to know if he can let the eastbound freight pass." The stationmaster looked at his watch and nodded. "Tell 'im to let 'em go," he said.

Gesturing with his thumb, the telegrapher reminded him, "You know, they'll be cutting it mightily close."

"They'll still make it on time. Tell Marcus to send the freight on through."

"All right," the telegrapher answered, and he began sending the message to the dispatcher in Marion.

"Tell 'im not to let nothin' else by, though," the stationmaster added, "That'll be the last train allowed to cross the line 'til after the funeral train is safely by here."

Cole looked around at the stationmaster and telegrapher. "You mean you have a freight coming through here?"

"In about half an hour," the stationmaster said with a nod. "Actually, it'll just be crossin' the main line about a mile north of here. It's a good thing, too. If it came through the station, most of the folks would think it was the funeral train instead of nothing but empty boxcars."

Cole turned back to examine the map again and found the cross track the stationmaster spoke of. He smiled. *All right, General Barlow*, he told himself. *Since you've found yourself an engine, I don't have any way to catch you unless I have one too. If you can steal one, so can I.*

Something woke Tamara. She lay in her berth for a few moments, feeling the gentle sway of the car and listening to the slow, measured clicks of the wheels passing over the rail joints. What was it that had awakened her? Was it an unusual sound? A dream? A sudden chill? She could not be sure...she only knew that she had not merely drifted awake but had been pulled from a deep sleep.

Tamara was in a lower berth, so she was able to lift the shade and peek through the window. It was still quite dark outside, and she saw no torches or bonfires to indicate that people were waiting along the track.

She lay back and closed her eyes again, but whatever had awakened her was now keeping her wide awake, so she decided to get up. Dressing in the close confines of the berth behind the curtains was not easy, but she had been doing it for two weeks and had gotten used to it. A moment later she parted the curtain and stepped onto the carpeted aisle.

A dim lantern burned at each end of the car. It was not bright enough to allow her to see much but provided enough light so that she could walk the length of the car without tripping. It was quiet in the car. All she could hear was the normal rush and rhythmic click of it traversing the rails. She glanced up and down the aisle and saw only the shadowy, dark-green drapes that hung over the berths behind which slept thirty-nine other passengers. Beneath the lantern at the rear of the car she saw the porter sitting in a chair that was tipped back against the wall. His hands were folded in his lap, and his chin was down on his chest. He, too, was sleeping.

Tamara moved noiselessly toward the rear, slipped past the porter, and left the car. Then she walked through the next two, which were equally dark and quiet, and continued on until she reached the last car on the train.

The front section of the funeral car was dark. As Tamara tiptoed through this section she heard the gentle snoring and even breathing of the general and admiral who were sleeping there. The middle section was brightly lit, and even though she had looked in here a half dozen times, something compelled her to step in again.

Tamara gasped. The coffin lid was normally closed while the train was under way. Tonight, however, it was open, and she discovered that she was staring right into Lincoln's face. She took a couple of steps toward the coffin and peered at him more closely than she had at any other time. It's amazing, she thought, how much he looks as if he's merely sleeping. His mouth was curled into the slightest suggestion of a smile.

Tamara had not seen the President until that night at Ford's Theater. She had seen pictures of him and, from those photographs, thought him a homely man. She had mentioned that to Matthew Faraday, and he discredited the pictures, saying, "No photograph could ever catch the infinite gradations of expression that passed over Lincoln's face each moment. Homely? Abraham Lincoln was one of the handsomest men I've ever met."

And now, even though those gradations of expression could no longer manifest themselves on his face, Tamara could see that the gentleness had remained. If only she had been able to look into his eyes. Despite herself, she felt her throat tighten and tears welling in her eyes. She turned away, only to see Admiral Davis standing just inside the door. Impulsively she hurried to him, and he embraced her, comforting her as if she were his own daughter.

"I...I'm so sorry," she stammered, "that I never knew him."

"Oh, but you do, my dear," the admiral whispered soothingly. "You and every man, woman, and child in this country know him. He has become a part of all of us."

A few moments later Tamara left the funeral car and returned to her berth. Whatever had been so disquieting to her earlier had passed. It was almost as if she had been compelled to look into Lincoln's face, and having done that, a wonderful feeling of peace came over her.

CHAPTER NINE

Cole Yeager dashed out of the Cardington Depot and onto the station platform, his mind whirling as he formulated a plan to catch up with General Earl Barlow and his men. He stopped short and looked around at the crowd standing under the gas lamps. Then, at the far end of the platform, he spotted the shadowy outline of what he was looking for—a storage shed—and he smiled. Walking quickly to the shed, he paused and looked over his shoulder at the darkened outlines of hundreds of people standing along the track waiting for the funeral train. As he had expected, everyone was staring down the track, watching anxiously for the first glimpse of the President's train.

He sidled up to the shed, tried the door, and found it locked. But lying on the ground beside the shed was a crowbar, and Cole used it to force open the door. He held the door open just long enough to spot a lantern hanging on a hook. Slipping inside the windowless shed, he grasped the lantern and pulled the door shut behind him.

Cole was thankful he always kept a matchbox in his

pocket for emergencies. He drew it out, struck a match, and lit the lantern. It took a few minutes of poking around before the agent found what he had been hoping to find: a box of railroad torpedoes. He had seen these explosive devices used by trackwalkers when he rode on troop trains during the war. Placed on railroad tracks, the torpedoes were set off when the wheels of the engine rode over them. The resulting loud noise was a signal to the engineer to make an emergency stop. That was exactly what Cole hoped to accomplish.

Grabbing three torpedoes, Cole slipped them in his pocket, extinguished the lantern, and stole out of the shed. Leaving his horse tethered at the depot, he then ran as quickly as he could along the twin lines of glimmering steel along the spur to the railroad junction one mile north of the station. He was relieved that it was far enough away from the depot and not on the main track so that no one waiting to watch the train pass would witness what he was about to do.

His pulse hammering in his head from the exertion of his run, he forced himself to breathe deeply and calm down. As his control returned, he scanned the countryside and listened intently. It was still quite dark, and the sounds of night creatures—frogs, crickets, an owl—were all he heard at first. Then another sound echoing in the distance reached him. It was the chugging of a steam engine, and he realized it had to be the eastbound freight.

Cole ran about a quarter of a mile up the cross track, then spread the three torpedoes out on the rail. Even as he worked, he could see the beam of the approaching headlamp stabbing through the night and hear the mournful sound of the whistle as the train drew closer. With the torpedoes in place, he scrambled away from the track into a clump of brush and watched the train approach.

Three sharp bangs sounded over the clatter of the train as

the wheels hit the torpedoes. Almost immediately the brakes squealed and shrieked, and steel slid on steel in a shower of sparks as the train came to a halt.

Cole stayed out of sight until the engineer and fireman climbed down from the cab to see what was wrong. From his hiding place, he could clearly hear them speaking to each other.

"What do you think it was?" the engineer asked.

"Well, it has to be that funeral train," his fireman replied. "But I thought we'd been given the go ahead on that."

"Maybe they speeded up the train."

The fireman pushed back his cap and scratched his forehead. "Then where is it? I sure don't see no lights, and I don't hear nothin', either."

Cole Yeager stepped out of his hiding place and walked toward the two men. "I'm sorry, gentlemen. I stopped your train."

The startled engineer jumped slightly, then whirled around to face the agent, illuminated by the glow of the headlamp. "You stopped it?" he cried. "What the hell for?" He glared at him. "This is no time for some fool joke!"

"I'm not joking," Cole replied coldly and pulled his pistol.

Dumbfounded, the two men immediately raised their hands. "Don't shoot us!" the fireman pleaded.

"I won't if you do as I say," the agent answered.

"Mister, you must be plumb crazy trying to rob this train," the engineer growled. "We're not hauling anything but some empty boxcars bound for Marion."

"I don't care what you're hauling. Disconnect your engine from them," Cole ordered.

"What?" exclaimed the engineer.

"All I want is your engine. Now uncouple it from the rest of the cars," Cole told him.

The fireman looked sharply at the engineer. "We better do it, Clyde. Anyone crazy enough to steal an engine by itself is crazy enough to do just about anything."

"Thank you for your cooperation, gentlemen," Cole replied, following them as they stumbled nervously toward the back of the engine.

The two men got to work pulling the connecting pins. Five minutes later, Cole signaled for them to step away from the track far enough to keep them from trying anything, but close enough for him to see them.

"Keep your hands up over your head...high," he called.

"Yes, sir, we're doin' it," the engineer replied.

Smiling to himself, Cole climbed into the engine where the hissing sound of steam and the dial on the gauge, illuminated by the cab's lantern, told him that the pressure was still high enough for him to make it move. He took one last glance at the two nervous trainmen, then opened the throttle, and within a moment the engine began rolling.

The last thing Cole had done prior to stopping the freight train was to set the switch at the junction so that, rather than cross the main line, his engine would turn south onto it. Minutes later, the engine Cole was driving pounded through the station at Cardington where the hundreds of people lining the platform all assumed it was the pilot engine for the funeral train. Within a few more moments he was away from Cardington, headed toward North Switch, where he hoped to catch up with General Barlow.

At North Switch Cole applied the brakes, and the engine rolled to a stop. He stuck his head out the cab and looked up and down the track, but he saw no sign of any other train. Where was Barlow? Was he on the main line or on the line headed for Marysville?

"Marysville," Cole said aloud.

Having no time to second-guess himself, he immediately

hopped down and turned the switch bar that would allow him to leave the main track. Then he climbed back into the engine, released the brake, and started rolling forward. As soon as the back wheels had cleared the switching point, he stopped the engine and ran back to the switch bar to close it. Then he hurried back to the cab and started toward Marysville.

On a siding halfway between Marysville and North Switch, General Earl Barlow climbed up into the engine he had stolen and saw by the lantern light that lit the dials a pistol pointed at him. Manley Daniels, Alan Tatterwall, and Lee Hawkins were standing in the cab, smirking.

"It was mighty thoughtful of you to send Evans and Posey on down to South Switch," Daniels drawled. "That makes our job of taking over a lot easier."

Barlow glared at him, his face incredulous. "Taking over? What are you talking about?" he demanded. "Colonel, what's the meaning of this?"

"Well, now, that's just the point, Barlow," Daniels replied. "I'm not a colonel anymore, and you aren't a general. So we got to talking about this, and we decided if we're going to steal Lincoln's body, we're going to do it for ourselves."

"Yeah," Alan Tatterwall put in, "why hold the body for somethin' we want the government to do? Why, afterward they could undo it just as pretty as you please, and we wouldn't have nothin'."

"That's where you're wrong," Barlow argued. "I believe the government would honor any agreement they made."

"You really think the Yankees are going to give me my slaves back?" Daniels asked.

"No," Barlow said. "I think slavery is finished forever...and I think in the long run we'll be glad this yoke has been lifted from our necks."

"This yoke, Barlow? Tell me, have you ever owned slaves?"

"No."

"Then you never meant to include the return of slavery in any bargain with the Yankee government, did you?"

Barlow shook his head firmly. "I had no intention whatever. All I seek is an honorable peace."

Daniels snorted derisively. "Yes well, I thought you might be thinking about something like that. Frankly, we don't care what kind of 'honorable' peace terms the government makes, because we don't plan to be here anyway. We're going to Canada—after we've collected one million dollars in ransom for Mr. Lincoln's body."

"One million dollars?" Barlow gasped.

"Yeah, it does take your breath away, doesn't it?" Daniels whispered his eyes gleaming. "But after seeing all these people turn out to view the body, we figure the government will pay that much to get it back."

"No!" Barlow cried. "No, I won't go along with that. I won't allow you to do it."

Tatterwall guffawed. "You hear that, Daniels? He won't allow us to do it!"

"Oh, I'm afraid you don't have anything at all to do with it now," Daniels replied.

"There are only three of you," Barlow reminded him. "You can't pull this off with just three men."

Daniels smiled. "Maybe not with your plan, but we can pull off the one I have in mind. You see, we're going to wreck the funeral train."

Barlow's face turned white. "You can't do that!" he cried. "Innocent people will get hurt!"

"Oh. You mean like the switchman back in Maryland? The one we killed?" Lee Hawkins asked.

"Killed?" the general gasped. He looked from one man to another. "You...you've already killed one man?"

"I'm afraid so, Barlow," Daniels answered. "So you see, it won't bother me to kill again."

"No, you can't—" Barlow began, but the butt of a pistol smashing the top of his head cut off his protest. Unconscious, the general slid from the train and down into the ditch beside the tracks.

The three men inside the cab gave the officer a final, ironic salute. Then they pushed the throttle forward and raced off into the night.

Cole Yeager saw the approaching headlight of an engine and realized that it was going the wrong way on the track heading for North Switch. He knew it had to be Barlow and that Barlow had to be after the funeral train. For a moment he was not sure what to do, and then a cold, calm understanding passed over him.

After first checking the steam pressure, Cole threw several more logs into the fire to keep it roaring and the pressure up. That done, he opened the throttle to full, increasing the speed to nearly fifty miles per hour.

With the train racing along the track toward the oncoming headlight, Cole climbed down the cab's steps and hung on. He looked at the ground rushing beneath him, moving so fast that it was all a blur, and shuddered. Then steeling himself, he took a deep breath and pushed himself away from the engine, leaping out as far as he could. He hit the ground with a bone-jarring thud, then tumbled and bounced painfully for several yards. Finally he rolled to a stop. Although every part of his body ached, he was sure nothing was broken.

Pulling himself to his feet, he watched, his heart pounding, as the two engines raced toward each other.

When Manley Daniels saw the headlamp of the engine barreling through the darkness toward him and realized what was about to happen, he screamed, "My God! Jump!"

Daniels was the first one out, with Tatterwall and Hawkins right behind him. The three men leapt from the engine on the opposite side of the- tracks from where Cole Yeager had landed. They were still bouncing along the ditch when the two engines collided.

The wrenching, shrieking sound of steel battering steel shattered the still night. Then a mighty explosion shook the ground as both boilers exploded, rocking the men who were now huddling in the ditch. A great column of steam soared to the darkened sky, and a scalding rain began to fall. Huge metal parts were flung into the air, then crashed back to the ground with the force of an artillery barrage.

Dorsey Evans and Buford Posey were nearing South Switch, where they intended to implement General Barlow's orders to block the track, when the explosion boomed into the night.

"What in the name of God was that?" Dorsey Evans exclaimed, turning around and staring back the way they had come.

Buford pointed at the towering fountain of steam, a luminous white cloud against the dark sky. "My God, Dorsey!" he cried. "I think the boiler on their engine exploded!"

"We better get back there and see if the general's all right," Dorsey declared, and, completely abandoning their intention to block the track, the two men raced back.

When the last piece of shrapnel had fallen and it was again safe to stand, Cole Yeager hauled himself out of the clump of bushes he had dived into for cover and looked at the mangled mountain of steel. The steam and shower of hot water had extinguished the boilers' flames, so there was no fire. Shattered boilers, crushed smokestacks, crumpled tenders, and broken wheels resting on twisted track were all that remained of the two great engines. Only the hissing steam still trapped in the cylinders and the snapping and popping of cooling metal could be heard in the night.

Drawing his gun, Cole moved slowly toward the wreck. It would have been impossible for anyone to survive the collision. For his own safety he had to assume that the men on board the other engine had jumped clear before it happened, and he began to search for them. But although he looked around carefully he saw and heard no one.

He reached the wreck, circled it warily, then checked the entire area. He could find neither survivors nor dead men. Deciding they must have eluded him by slipping back the way they had come, he started up the track.

Dawn was just beginning to break as Cole headed toward Cardington. He had gone about a quarter of a mile from the wreck when he saw three men walking toward him, one of them gingerly rubbing the top of his head. Realizing that they had not yet seen him, he scurried into some trackside brush and hid until they were practically in front of him. Then he leapt from his hiding place, leveled his pistol, and confronted them.

"All right, you three, drop your gun belts," he ordered.

Cole's abrupt appearance evidently startled the three men, because they peered at him in shocked surprise. Two of them started to comply with his demand, but one man hesitated, as if he were ready to make a play for his weapon.

"No, Dorsey," Earl Barlow commanded, holding his hand out toward the man. "He has us dead to rights."

"That was a wise order, General," Cole commented with a slow nod. Then he appraised the man he had been dogging for so long, and said, "Well, it looks like your little scheme is over."

"I guess it is," Barlow agreed, sighing loudly. "Did you find any bodies in the wreckage?"

"No."

The general's eyebrows shot up. "Then, Colonel Yeager, I'm afraid it isn't over after all."

"What do you mean?"

"I was the victim of a mutiny," he began. "Colonel Manley Daniels and two of his men hit me, threw me from the cab, and took the engine. They are planning to wreck the funeral train. You see, we originally planned to steal Lincoln's body for political reasons—to gain concessions for the South, but now he intends to hold the body for ransom money and, once he gets it, leave the country. Since you found no bodies in the wreckage, we must assume that Daniels and his men got away."

"Why should I believe you?" Cole demanded.

"Yes, indeed, why should you?" Barlow replied wearily. He sighed and looked up at Cole. "I do give you my word as a fellow officer and a gentleman." He gestured at the two men with him. "In any event, I can assure you that these men and I are no longer a threat. But the threat still exists from Manley Daniels and his men." Cole was thoughtful for a long moment, then asked, "How far is it to Marysville?"

"It's about three miles back," the general answered. "Why?"

"I've got to get there in time to send a telegram to Cardington before the funeral train gets there. If Daniels plans on making yet another attempt to steal the President's body, it's likely that he'll try it there," Cole explained.

Dorsey Evans abruptly stepped beside the two officers and looked at his commander. "General, I know a way to do it if you really want to help this fella," he said.

"Yes, Dorsey, I am prepared to help him in any way I can," Barlow assured him. "Now, what is this way you know?"

"Well, sir, there's a handcart about half a mile up the track. He could make it in time with that."

"Yes," Barlow agreed, "he could. Come on, Colonel, we'll help."

"Why are you so interested in helping me?" Cole asked pointedly.

The general shook his head in disgust. "Because I just found out that Daniels killed a switchman in Maryland. And while I realize my helping you now will not lessen my culpability for that man's death, I don't want to see any more innocent people hurt. I planned this mission very carefully to avoid any such casualties. I'll be damned if I let that traitorous bastard turn this into a scheme for his own profit now!"

Cole nodded, then peered at the two men working with Barlow.

"If the General says help you, Colonel, I'll die tryin'," Dorsey promised.

"Me, too," Buford Posey echoed.

Cole slipped his pistol back into its holster and looked at Barlow. "All right, General, let's go."

Breaking into an easy trot, the four men moved quickly up the track until they came to the handcart Dorsey had mentioned sitting beside the rail bed. They set the cart on the track, then with two of them on one side of the pump handle and two on the other, they got the cart moving at a very fast clip. It took less than fifteen minutes to make it to Marysville, and there, accepting Barlow's verbal bond that he and his two men would not escape, Cole went into the telegraph office. He had the telegrapher send a coded wire to Cardington for delivery to Matthew Faraday on board the funeral train, warning him that danger might be imminent.

As the funeral train chugged through the station at a pace that was only a little faster than a brisk walk, the telegram was gotten on board and delivered to Faraday without the train having to stop. The silver-haired detective read the telegram, then put it in his pocket and went on into the lavatory to attend to his morning ablutions. He was just stropping his razor when Jonas Ward stepped into the small room and began making his own preparations to shave.

"Good morning, Mr. Ward," Faraday said.

"Faraday," Ward replied, then began laying out his shaving equipment. "I'm glad to see that you've behaved as a mourner on this trip." he went on.

Faraday looked at Ward's reflection in the mirror. "That's the purpose of my being here," he answered lightly. Wetting his shaving brush, he began to work up a lather in his mug.

"Yes, well, I must confess that I was a little concerned when I first saw you," Ward admitted with a nod. "I am the one in charge of all the security arrangements, and I don't want—or need—any help."

"Oh, I quite agree," Faraday assured him, smiling.

The two men lapsed into silence for a few moments. They each steadied themselves to move with the rocking train and cautiously began using their straight razors.

"As you can see," Ward finally said, "this entire trip has been without incident because I've made certain nothing could go wrong."

"And I'm sure all the citizens are grateful to you," Faraday said.

Ward nodded his thanks and continued shaving. "Of course, there was that unpleasant incident in Philadelphia," he went on, "but that wasn't my fault. That was the fault of the Philadelphia police. Their forces were totally inadequate to handle that crowd when the rioting began."

"Yes, well, a few pickpockets can cause a great deal of difficulty," Faraday said, his face somber. "In fact, since the discussion has taken this direction, I should pass on some information I just received."

"Yes, I saw that a telegram was delivered to you this morning," Ward told him.

Faraday laughed. "And, ever the policeman, you managed to time your shave so as to find out what it was about. Am I correct?"

"If you have any information regarding this train and its security, it is your duty to share it," Ward snapped, clearly not finding any humor in the situation.

Unruffled, Faraday shook his head. "It's not that I want to hide the information from you, you understand," he assured him evenly. "It's just that, well, the information is from an over-zealous colleague of mine who has perhaps misunderstood my reason for being on this train. And, besides, it may be nothing at all."

"Suppose you tell me what it is and let me make that decision," Ward demanded impatiently.

"Very well," Faraday said. "One of my agents in Cleveland has notified me that he has information several pickpockets are heading for Columbus with the intention of working the crowd there. As I said, it's probably nothing, but..."

"What do you mean, nothing?" Ward grated. He held his finger up in admonishment. "Mr. Faraday, this very discussion demonstrates to me the difference between the amateurishness of a private detective, such as you, and the professionalism of a public officer, such as myself. In my long experience I have learned to follow up on all leads and clues. If we have the slightest hint that pickpockets may be at work in Columbus, then I intend to proceed as if this will absolutely be the case. If we err, we lose nothing to err on the side of caution. I shall send a telegram to the Columbus police department telling them to be extra vigilant. Did your agent say how these pickpockets might arrive?"

"Perhaps by train," Faraday suggested.

"Very well. Then I shall order that any train arriving before us be stopped and thoroughly searched."

"If you think that's best," agreed Faraday with a slight shrug. Then he diligently finished shaving and neatly put his equipment in his case. "I'm just glad I don't have the responsibility that's on your shoulders," he told Jonas Ward as he stepped out of the lavatory.

Tucking his shaving kit under his arm, Faraday smiled to himself and returned to his car. He found that the porter had already converted his berth into a seat, and Tamara Goodnight was sitting there waiting for him, staring pensively out the window.

"You're up early this morning," Faraday told her brightly.

Tamara turned toward him, her lovely face reflective. "Yes, I suppose I am," she replied without elaborating. "You received a telegram this morning; was it from Cole?"

"Yes," he said softly, glancing around to see that no one was eavesdropping. Satisfied they were not being overheard, he went on. "He's caught some of the men, but there's still a group determined to finish the job. He was afraid they might have tried something in Cardington, but apparently they didn't have enough time to put any plan into effect. Perhaps they will in Columbus. The problem is, we will be in Columbus before Cole, so we'll be on our own."

"Do you have any idea what we should do?" Tamara asked.

Faraday chuckled. "Well, I just arranged for Mr. Ward to help us," he told her, his bright blue eyes dancing, "though he doesn't realize what he's doing."

Tamara tilted her head and smiled up at him. "And just how have you done that?"

Faraday explained that he had suggested there might be pickpockets arriving in Columbus to work the crowd as they had in Philadelphia. If the Columbus police took particular care to investigate all incoming passengers, suspecting each one of being a pickpocket, they might accidentally turn up Daniels and his men. And if not, such a flurry of police activity would certainly make things more difficult for the would-be body snatchers.

"In the meantime," he added, rising from his seat as he prepared to make his way back to the funeral car, "I don't intend to let the President's coffin out of my sight."

It seemed to Tamara that the city of Columbus had amassed a greater profusion of flowers to honor the slain President than any other city. Matthew Faraday and she were riding in a carriage as part of the funeral parade. The people lining the streets held roses that they tossed under the wheels of the hearse as it came by. The invalid soldiers from the veterans' hospital had literally covered the street for several hundred yards approaching and leaving the hospital with lilac blooms that were crushed by the wheels of the hearse as they rode over them.

The coffin was carried into the state capitol's rotunda and placed on a catafalque that was unlike all the others. Rather than being covered with black velvet, it was laden with moss, fresh green leaves, white roses, and orange blossoms. When the coffin was set into the soft bed, it crushed the flowers so that an almost cloyingly sweet scent was released into the vast hall.

Watching the funeral procession from a street corner near the state capitol, Colonel Manley Daniels signaled in disgust for his two men to leave. As the threesome departed, he whispered to them, "I don't know what it is, but the police here seem awful watchful. We're going to have to try somewhere else."

"We're runnin' out of places to try," Alan Tatterwall

reminded him. "Hell, they'll have this decayin' mummy in Springfield in another couple of days."

Daniels glared at the man; "Don't you think I know that?" he snarled. "Don't worry. If we don't get him before then, we'll get him there. We've come this, far, and I don't intend to turn back now."

CHAPTER TEN

EARL BARLOW, FORMER BRIGADIER GENERAL OF THE Confederate Army, was sitting on a bench at the far end of the wooden platform of the depot in Marysville, leaning against a lantern post. As he watched Dorsey Evans and Buford Posey play a game of mumblety-peg, he suddenly realized that what had once been a command of thousands of men had been reduced to just these two. He who had led great armies to battle now had only Sergeant Dorsey Evans and Private Buford Posey to lead—and they, like he, were the prisoners of Colonel Cole Yeager.

Barlow was taking himself to task, asking himself what had possessed him to have ever conceived this last, desperate idea in the first place. What had he really hoped to gain? Had he honestly thought the Union government would deal with him in return for Abraham Lincoln's corpse? How that the war was over, there were no Union or Confederate governments, just one federal government. Even if the North had agreed to deal, whom would they deal with? The Confederacy was no more; the officials were scattered, and there was no organization left. And even if he had successfully pulled off the theft, he would have been regarded not as a commanding officer of a beleaguered nation but as a criminal against society.

Disgusted with himself, Barlow pinched the bridge of his nose and shook his head. On the battlefield he had seen men, fatigued and shocked by the rigors and horrors of war, make irrational judgments. He had seen brave men do cowardly things and meek, mild-mannered men do things of great courage. Barlow was convinced that these acts stemmed from a type of lunacy brought on by war, and he had even talked with battle surgeons about it and learned they agreed with him.

Now he wondered whether he was suffering from this battle madness. Could it be that he had seen too much war and, combining that with the loss of all he held dear with the South's defeat, had been driven to lunacy? Was this what had driven him to the insane idea of plotting the theft of Abraham Lincoln's body?

His grim musing was interrupted when he suddenly realized that Dorsey Evans was standing over him, clearing his throat. He looked up and said, "I'm sorry, Dorsey. Did you say something?"

"Yes, I did, General. That fella— what did you say his name was?"

"Yeager. Colonel Cole Yeager."

"Yes, sir. Well, me and Buford was wonderin' what he's doin' right now."

Barlow glanced back toward the depot building. "He apparently has a contact on board the funeral train. And now he's wiring him to see if the train arrived in Columbus without incident." Dorsey looked thoughtful for a moment, then asked quietly, "General, what if the three of us was to just light out now? We could be gone by the time he comes back outside. Hell, we ain't got nothin' holdin' us here."

"We have my word of honor holding us here," Barlow replied sternly. "Don't forget, I gave the man my word that we wouldn't leave."

"But he's a Yankee!" Dorsey exclaimed.

"My word is my word, no matter whom I give it to," the general told him firmly.

Nodding slowly, Dorsey said, "All right. If you say so, sir. I was just askin', that's all."

"Here he comes now," Buford Posey announced, and Barlow turned to see Cole Yeager walking down the platform toward them.

As Cole reached the three men, he looked at their tired, expectant faces and then sat down next to Barlow on the bench. "The train made it to Columbus without any trouble," he told them. "Before they arrived, Matthew Faraday, my contact on the funeral train, had tipped off the Columbus police that pickpockets were coming in from out of town. Apparently the police watched everyone so closely that your man Daniels didn't have a chance to try anything."

Barlow's blue eyes narrowed. "He isn't my man anymore," he reminded Cole in a steely voice.

"No, I guess he isn't," Cole agreed.

"Colonel Yeager..."

Cole held out his hand to stop the general from saying any more. "Actually, I'm an agent for the Faraday Security Service," he explained. "I'm not a colonel anymore."

Barlow sighed. "Nor am I a general," he mumbled. "Though I guess the idea is going to take some getting used to. At any rate, whatever your official capacity is at the moment, I'm surrendering my men and myself to you. You may do with us as you please, though I beg of you to consider the fact that neither Sergeant...that is, Mr. Evans—" he corrected himself "—nor Mr. Posey had anything to do with, nor did they even know about, the murder of the switchman back in Maryland."

"Hell, General, you didn't know nothin' about it neither 'til yesterday," Dorsey quickly spoke up, defending the former officer.

"It doesn't matter," Barlow insisted with a weary shake of his head. "I was in command of the operation, so that makes me responsible for anything that happened as a result of it."

Cole rubbed his chin as he regarded the men who had just placed themselves in his custody. The truth was, he had no idea what he should do with them. He could not very well arrest them for conspiracy to steal Lincoln's body. The Secretary of War had specifically ordered that this operation be kept secret to avoid creating a scandal. To arrest them on that charge would shatter that secret. The only other, charge would be in connection with the death of the switchman. And looking at them now he believed them when they said they knew nothing about it. He could see clearly they were horrified by it.

Cole gazed at the rolling countryside for several moments as he weighed the problem. Then he turned to the former officer and declared, "General Barlow, the way I see this, you are only in command of something if the men follow your orders. It's obvious that Manley Daniels isn't following your orders now, and he probably wasn't following them back in Maryland either. He was acting as a renegade when he murdered that switchman, so I can't see how you were responsible for that man's death."

Averting his face, Barlow stood up and brushed the seat of his trousers. "That's...that's a very generous way of looking at it," he said in a hoarse voice. "And I appreciate it. But the fact remains, we are your prisoners."

"No," Cole countered. "No, you're not. Just give me your word that you won't try to steal the President's body again, and I'll have no reason to treat you as a prisoner."

Barlow pulled himself to his full height and squared his shoulders. Then he turned and looked at Cole solemnly. "You have my word, sir," he intoned.

"And mine," Dorsey put in.

"Mine, too," Buford added.

"Then, gentlemen, the war is over," Cole said softly, "and my suggestion to you is...go home."

A pained, faraway look came into Dorsey's eyes. "Home?" he asked. "Where is that, Colonel?"

"Georgia, Alabama, Virginia—wherever you came from," Cole replied airily.

"I think what he means is that for many of our men, there is no home left," Barlow explained softly.

Cole looked into the former sergeant's eyes and shook his head slowly. "I'm sorry, Dorsey. I truly am."

Dorsey shrugged. "That's the fortunes of war, I guess, Colonel," he said, accepting the apology. He smiled silently for a moment, then went on, "Anyway, I appreciate what you're doin' for us, and I'll get goin' afore you change your mind." He turned to his commanding officer and asked, "General? You ready to leave?"

For a moment Barlow looked thoughtfully at the two men and finally said, "Actually, Dorsey, I think I won't be going back with you and Buford just yet." He turned and smiled crookedly at Cole. "Tell me, Mr. Yeager, does my freedom mean I am also free to go with you?"

"With me?"

"Yes. I want to help you stop Daniels," he explained. "Oh, I appreciate your telling me that I am not responsible for what he did back in Maryland, but I don't entirely agree with you. I feel responsible for that, and I feel responsible for anything that turncoat may do from here on out. You see, when I surrendered to you, I wasn't just surrendering myself and the two men with me, I was surrendering the entire scheme—and I intend to see that it is stopped. The only way I can do that is to stop Daniels. The best way to do that would be to help you."

"General, what about us?" Dorsey asked. He raised his eyebrows inquiringly at Buford Posey, and the blue-eyed, shy man nodded eagerly. "There's three of them now, and we know what they look like. We'd be a big help. Can't we be a part of this?"

Barlow turned to Dorsey and Buford and studied them thoughtfully. Then he put a fatherly hand on each man's shoulder. "We fought a long war, and for all that time Lincoln was our enemy. Can you really put aside those feelings so quickly?"

Dorsey and Buford looked at each other for a long moment, then they nodded. "General," Dorsey said, "the way we see it, Daniels is wrong. And those men with him are criminals. You've always been an honorable man, that's why we respect you. We can't let you do this alone."

Barlow glanced at Cole, who nodded slightly and smiled. Then the general's eyes grew red, and he turned away and coughed. A moment later when he looked back at his two men, he was smiling. "Dorsey, Buford, I can always use two good men," he said softly.

Barlow turned back to the Faraday agent. He took a deep breath and said, "Now it's up to you, Mr. Yeager."

Cole silently assessed the three men. Then he smiled and shook hands with each of them. "My name is Cole," he replied warmly. "And I'll be honored to have you with me."

Barlow grinned. "And I would be pleased if you would call me Earl."

"I'll be damned," cried Dorsey, laughing. "What is it? Something funny about my name?"

"No, sir, I don't guess so," Dorsey replied sheepishly. "It's just that I never knew generals had first names."

Barlow laughed heartily. Then he turned to Cole. "You're the man in charge, tell me what you want to do."

"Very well, Earl," Cole said with a nod. "Why don't you tell me if you have any idea where Daniels might strike next."

Barlow stared pensively at the planks of the platform for a few moments. Then he looked at Cole, a knowing expression on his face. "Our backup plan, in case no opportunity presented itself earlier, was to wait until the body was interred in Springfield and then steal it."

Surprised at the notion. Cole gave a long whistle. "Of course!" he exclaimed. "How ingenious. Once the President was buried, no one would ever suspect there would be further trouble." He took out his watch and checked the time, then looked back at Barlow. "The funeral train isn't scheduled to depart from Columbus until eight o'clock tonight. We'll catch the next westbound train and be there before it leaves."

The four men caught up with the funeral train just before it pulled out of the Columbus railroad station. Not seeing Matthew Faraday on the platform Cole told Barlow and his men to wait in the depot. He then moved through the passenger cars until he found him sitting alone reading the evening newspaper. Faraday followed Cole into the depot to where the three men were waiting nervously. After introducing Faraday to General Barlow, Cole told him all that had occurred, including how Barlow had come to surrender himself, and that he and his men were now offering their services to stop Manley Daniels.

"We heard about the train wreck," Faraday told Cole, "something about a couple of stolen engines." He paused and smiled. "The authorities believe the whole thing was done by drunken soldiers, either in some sort of celebration of the end of the war or as a rather macabre salute to President Lincoln. As far as I know, no one has linked the accident with any attempt to steal the President's body."

Cole's shoulders sagged in relief. "Thank God for that," he said, then added, "Mr. Faraday, if you can make the arrangements, I thought it might be a good idea if we joined the train for the final leg of the journey."

Faraday looked thoughtfully at the three newcomers, and his craggy face twisted into a frown. "I certainly see the advantage to having three men with us who can identify Daniels and his men," he said. "But you know Jonas Ward will be a problem. Just a minute. Let me think."

The detective stepped away from the men and began to pace up and down the depot. Finally he stopped and, grinning broadly, walked back to Cole.

"All right," he said, his blue eyes twinkling, "this is what we'll do. Dorsey Evans and Buford Posey, I will arrange for you to ride in the staff's car as relief trainmen. Earl Barlow, you and Cole will have to ride with me. If Ward questions it, and I'm sure he will, I'll convince him that you're on some assignment for me and that I needed to confer with you."

As each man nodded his acceptance, Faraday smiled at him. "All right, gentlemen. We'd best arrange this." The detective turned and led the foursome to the train. They stopped first at the car the staff rode in. After settling Dorsey and Buford in, Faraday walked through the train to his own car with Cole and Barlow trailing behind. When he reached his seat, he turned and looked his young agent over. "Cole, I'd say you might enjoy a chance to wash up and change your clothes. We've stored your traveling bag in the luggage car. Shall I send the porter for it?"

Cole rubbed the stubble on his jaw, then pushed open his

greatcoat and looked down at his soiled suit. "I can't think of anything I'd rather do," he admitted. "Unfortunately, this is my only suit, so I'm afraid I won't look very dignified."

Faraday laughed. "Never mind that. The important thing is that you're here." Noticing that Cole was glancing around the car, he commented, "I assume you're wondering where Miss Goodnight is?"

Cole grinned sheepishly. "You're right, Mr. Faraday."

Faraday smiled at the young man, then gestured toward the front of the train. "She's spending time with some of the other women on board. But you'll see her soon, don't worry. We'll be dining shortly, and she'll be joining us." Then he turned to the general. "Barlow, we're about the same size. Perhaps I can lend you a change of clothing."

The general started to protest, "Mr. Faraday, really, that's far too kind an offer, and—"

"I wouldn't have made it if I didn't mean it," Faraday interrupted. "Come, gentlemen. I'll see to arranging a couple of berths and get you squared away at the same time."

"Thank you, sir," Barlow murmured, then followed Faraday and Cole. He rubbed his chin, which was badly in need of a shave. "It has been a few days since I was able to clean up. I, too, would welcome the opportunity."

At that moment the train lurched forward, and the three men stumbled slightly at the sudden movement. Cole drew his watch from his vest pocket, then looked at Barlow and smiled. "Right on time," he noted. "It's just eight o'clock. We're on our way to Indianapolis."

Shortly before nine o'clock, Tamara Goodnight appeared at the door to the dining car. Cole, who had been waiting impatiently for her arrival since he had sat down at the table with Matthew Faraday and Earl Barlow, saw her instantly. As he watched her glide down the aisle toward them, Cole was certain that she had grown more beautiful during the last few days. Her copper-colored hair, cascading in ringlets to her shoulders, softly framed her face. She was wearing the same green velvet gown she had worn to Ford's Theater the night Lincoln was shot. Smiling radiantly when she spotted him, she quickened her step. Cole rose and pulled out the chair on his right, and she slipped gracefully into her seat. Earl Barlow and Matthew Faraday sat opposite them.

As if by tacit agreement, none of them discussed the plot to steal the President's body, and—at least for this one evening—they behaved as if they were old friends enjoying each other's company over a delicious dinner. However, at the end of the meal, as they were making their way to the passenger car, Barlow suddenly stopped short, and a pained expression crossed his face.

"Earl, is something wrong?" Cole asked.

"No," Barlow murmured, gazing into the younger man's eyes and smiling weakly. "No, nothing is wrong. I'm just wondering if I have any right to be here, that's all."

Faraday put his hand on Barlow's shoulder. "We are all on the same side now, my friend," he assured him. "You have as much right as anyone."

During the slow night run from Columbus, Ohio, to Indianapolis, Indiana, the trackside was thronged with people. Great bonfires lit the skies, allowing Tamara to look through the window and see the large crowds gathered at every crossing. However, very few passengers on board the funeral train witnessed these outpourings of respect for Abraham Lincoln. Almost as soon as the dining car was closed, most of the passengers asked the porters to prepare their berths, anticipating rising early for the next scheduled stop at seven in the morning. The lamps were extinguished, and only the dimmed lanterns at the ends of the cars remained lit.

Cole walked Tamara to her seat, and they discovered that her berth had not yet been prepared; Matthew Faraday was accompanying Earl Barlow to his accommodations in the car just forward. He left his two younger companions, telling them diplomatically that he welcomed the opportunity to speak about the war with a Southern general. Bidding Tamara good night and telling Cole they would see him later, the two men excused themselves and left the car.

Cole was grateful to Faraday, because he was certain the real purpose his employer had taken Barlow aside was to allow Tamara and him the opportunity to be alone for a while. Of course, they were not actually alone. There were a number of other passengers in the car, mostly congressmen.

"Can you believe it?" Cole heard one of the congressmen ask loudly. "For the rest of the trip, the engineer has been ordered not to pass any station at a speed greater than five miles per hour. At this rate, it'll take forever to get to Springfield!"

"Not only that," someone else said, "but I would be willing to wager that we are stopped at least twice during the night by people who want to present bouquets of flowers. More flowers, for God's sake! It's as if everyone in the country with nothing more than a petunia has conceived the same idea."

Cole and Tamara glanced at each other, and Cole frowned. "They sound rather cynical," he whispered.

"I'm sure they're just weary," Tamara breathed, her face softening in compassion. "After all, it's been a long and tiring journey for them."

"It's been just as long and tiring for you," Cole reminded her, "and you're not complaining that way."

Tamara smiled. "I'm younger than they are," she said gently. "Besides, there were many campaigns during the war when I was just as tired as I am now, and I learned not to let it bother me." She glanced out the window, then looked back at Cole. "Since they haven't had to deal with such a thing before, I feel a certain tolerance for their increasing irritability."

"You are a nicer person than I am," Cole admitted. "When I think of the millions of people who would give anything to be in the position these men are in right now, I have little patience for their complaints."

The sound of snoring erupted from a passenger who was asleep in the front of the car. Slightly startled, Cole then chuckled. "Well, at least one of them seems to have adapted," he quipped. "Then of course, I suppose if you can sleep during a session of congress—as I understand many of these gentlemen do—you can sleep anywhere."

As Tamara laughed the train made a sharp turn, and she was forced to lean against Cole. The young agent looked down at her quickly, as if to reassure her that it was not his doing. But looking at her was a mistake, for he suddenly found himself staring deeply into her amber eyes and feeling that he was looking into her soul. Cole sensed that Tamara wanted desperately to look away to prevent him from seeing more than she thought he should see, but she could not. It was as though they were held together by some strange hypnotic power. Then the train straightened its path, and there was no longer a reason for her to be leaning against him. She tried halfheartedly to pull away, but Cole stopped her by putting his arm around her. She did not protest the move.

They sat that way for a long, quiet moment, staring at each other, but saying nothing.

A sudden, brilliant display appeared outside the darkened window as a shower of sparks flew by, flared for an instant, then died. Most of the congressmen had piled into their berths, and their snores were underscored by the rhythmic clackety-clack of the wheels. Cole was aware of these things, yet none of them mattered. The closeness of

Tamara's lips to his had mesmerized him. Gradually, so slowly as to be imperceptible, he inched closer to her. She sat completely still as if unable to move or speak as he drew closer. Finally he was so close that he could feel her breath upon his lips.

"Cole?" she murmured fearfully.

"I love you, Tamara," he answered softly.

Instantly he felt her relax; her tension and resistance melted. She moved to meet him and close the small distance between them.

The kiss was so hungry and urgent that they might have been alone in the wilderness—not in a darkened car filled with people. It went on and on, growing more forceful and passionate.

Finally Cole pulled away from Tamara and looked at her. Her eyes were open, and in the shadows her face appeared expressionless. Suddenly he was afraid she was angry.

"Tamara," he gasped. "Please, you must forgive me! I...I had no right. And besides, this would hardly be either the time or the place to..."

She put a finger on his lips to silence him. "Cole...did you mean what you said...just before you kissed me?" she stammered, her voice anxious.

"That I love you?"

She nodded. "Yes. Did you mean it?"

"I meant it with all my heart," he whispered hoarsely.

"Then don't apologize," she said with a smile. He felt her body relax, as if his words had erased her fears. "When this journey is over, we'll find the proper time and place."

Cole returned her smile, relieved that she was not angry with him. He raised her hand to his lips and kissed it. "Oh, yes, I promise you...we will find the proper time and the proper place." He stood up and looked down at her. "But it isn't now, and it isn't here." Kissing her hand one more time, he told her softly, "I should go now. We've got a long day ahead of us."

"Good night," she whispered.

He gave her a smile, then turned and headed toward the next car to join Faraday and Barlow. He was so light-headed and giddy that it took all his self-control not to dance down the aisle. Controlling his feelings, fie reminded himself that he was on a funeral train and that, although he was jubilant, everyone else on board was somber.

When Cole entered the next car, he immediately noticed the dim glow of lantern light spilling into the otherwise darkened aisle between the berths and knew that he would find Faraday and Barlow waiting for him there. Sighs and snores resonated around him, telling him that the other passengers were already asleep. After riding on the funeral train for two weeks, they had become so accustomed to the passing displays of mourning as well as the discomfort of life on board that their senses were numbed. Recalling Tamara's words, Cole smiled to himself as he realized how right she had been. He sighed and moved toward the pool of light in the middle of the car.

Cole murmured a greeting when he reached the two men, then sat beside them. In silence they stared through the window at the people, the bonfires, and the other displays as well as at the incessant rain.

"If I thought this rain would discourage Daniels, I would welcome it," Faraday finally said. "But I'm sure it'll make no more difference to him than it does to those poor souls who are standing out there in the downpour in the middle of the night, just waiting for a glimpse of the train as it goes by."

Cole turned to the former general. "Earl, when do you think Daniels will try again?"

Barlow shook his head slowly. "I'm sure he has no idea that I've thrown in with you, so he would have no reason to suspect that you would know of the backup plan we made." He looked intently at the two agents. "I believe he will resort to that plan now."

"And the backup plan is the one you mentioned earlier?" Faraday asked.

"That's correct. He'll wait until the actual interment at Springfield, and then he'll rob the grave."

"All right," Cole said resolutely. "Then that's where we'll get him."

As the train pulled into the Indianapolis depot the next morning, the rain was coming down harder than it had at any time during the entire trip. Believing it would eventually stop, the city fathers and planners of the parade postponed the procession until the afternoon.

However, the rain did not stop; in fact, it intensified. The downpour rushed through the streets in rivulets. The crepe bunting that had been hung on nearly every house drooped limply, and the black dye ran in dark trickles down the fronts of the buildings.

Finally the procession was canceled, and it was decided that all the allotted time would be used to allow the people to view the body. The hearse was backed up to the funeral car, and Lincoln's coffin was loaded on board to be taken to the statehouse.

When the viewing was over, the coffin was taken back to the train, moving through the great, silent throngs who stood in the rain and watched. There were no funeral dirges, no muffled drums, no measured footfalls of marching soldiers, no firing of guns. Only the hollow clop of the horses' hooves and the quiet rolling of the hearse's wheels broke the unearthly silence. As Cole Yeager stood watching, he felt a chill at the sight of so many people standing so quietly. He would not have thought it possible that in a crowd of over one hundred thousand people you would be able to hear a pin drop.

The hearse reached the depot, and the President's coffin was reloaded on the train. After a brief prayer the funeral train once again chugged westward with its precious cargo, leaving Indianapolis behind. Now all that remained of the sorrowful journey was the state of Illinois, the ceremonies in Chicago, and the final interment in Springfield.

Later that night, after Cole had dined with Matthew Faraday, Tamara Goodnight, and Earl Barlow, he made his way to the lavatory to wash up before going to sleep. As he walked through the car, trying hard to stifle his yawns, he saw on virtually every face he passed a weariness that came not only from the long and exhausting journey, but also from more than two weeks of unending grief and sorrow. Every passenger seemed glad that the ordeal was soon to end. Cole was glad it was nearly over, too. He only hoped that their secret mission would be concluded successfully.

He decided to find Earl Barlow and go over things with him one more time, just to make certain that Manley Daniels would not have any surprises for them. Cole searched the car for the former general, and when he could not find him, he grew apprehensive. For a moment he was afraid Barlow might have gone back on his word.

Heading toward the rear of the train, Cole set out to find him, but he was unsuccessful until he reached the vestibule between the last passenger car and the funeral car. There he found Barlow, holding on to one of the steel poles that ran from the floor to the overhanging roof of the car. The older man was looking out at the passing countryside and the people who stood singly, in family units, and in larger groups under torches or around blazing camp fires just for a fleeting glimpse of the train as it came by.

"Oh, here you are," Cole murmured.

Barlow turned to look at Cole, and the agent was shocked to see the general's face streaked with tears. Instantly he regretted interrupting the general's reverie. Neither man said anything for a long moment, then Barlow whispered, "My God. To think I would have robbed the world of this opportunity to express its sorrow. We must stop Daniels...We must."

CHAPTER ELEVEN

AT 11:00 A.M. ON MONDAY, MAY 1, THE FUNERAL TRAIN arrived in Chicago. As soon as the ceremonies surrounding the unloading of Lincoln's coffin were concluded, the Faraday team took great precautions to avoid Jonas Ward and his security men and disembarked from the train. They made their way to a quiet corner of the depot to hear Matthew Faraday outline the strategy for protecting Lincoln's body. The detective knew that Chicago, not to be outdone by New York or Philadelphia, would stage the most elaborate funeral put on by any of the cities. As a result, he had been very thorough in devising his plan to protect Lincoln.

Faraday believed Earl Barlow, Dorsey Evans, and Buford Posey made fine additions to the team. During the train trip from Columbus he had spent several hours with Earl Barlow and discovered that Cole's original assessment of him was accurate. Barlow was an unusually honorable man, guided by the highest principles. Faraday was firmly convinced that Barlow was now dedicated to stopping Daniels. While he had not spent any time with Dorsey and

186

Buford who were laying low in the staff car, he confidently accepted Barlow's word that the Tennesseans were trustworthy.

Prior to Barlow's surrender, Cole Yeager was the only Faraday agent who could identify any of the would-be kidnappers, and even then his knowledge was limited to Earl Barlow's appearance. Now that the three Southerners were working with them and could readily identify Manley Daniels, Lee Hawkins, and Alan Tatterwall, the team had an advantage that Faraday welcomed. And because Chicago would not be outdone, he knew the challenge would be even greater here than before.

As in other cities, the Chicago newspapers had published the funeral cortege route in advance to ensure that a large crowd would turn out to honor the slain President. Faraday decided that each of the Southerners would position them-selves along the route with one of his agents. Cole Yeager would be paired with Buford Posey, Tamara Goodnight with Earl Barlow, and Faraday himself joined Dorsey Evans. Once the cortege had reached the Court House and the twenty-four-hour viewing period began, the teams would rotate the watch every four hours, allowing two pairs to rest while the third kept vigil.

When the Southerners wholeheartedly endorsed the plan, Faraday was pleased. They agreed to meet on the front steps of the Court House at the end of the procession, and the teams moved off to assume their positions along the parade route.

However, none of the teams spotted Daniels and his men during the procession. The long vigil in the Court House began uneventfully as well, and Matthew Faraday and Dorsey Evans retired the first shift without a mishap. Leaving Dorsey to keep watch, Faraday came into the judges' chambers, where the team was resting, to awaken Earl

Barlow and Tamara Goodnight who were to take the second shift.

"Tamara," Cole mumbled sleepily from his chair, "let me take this shift. It's after midnight."

"No, Cole," Tamara replied, standing stiffly next to Earl Barlow in the doorway. "I want to do this. Throughout this ordeal you have ridden in the cold rain and suffered through long sleepless nights. This is the least I can do."

"But, Tamara...if Daniels and his men show up at all it will be tonight...in the darkest hours...I don't want you in that sort of danger. They almost killed innocent people in..." His tired voice trailed off.

Tamara sighed softly, and a small smile played at her lips. She walked over to the chair on which Cole was sprawled and placed her hand lightly on his tousled dark hair. "Sleep, Cole," she whispered soothingly. "Earl Barlow certainly knows how to handle a situation like this. And if he spots them, I promise I'll waken you at once." The lanky young man was too tired to argue with the determined nurse anymore. He nodded sleepily and closed his eyes. Tamara tiptoed to the door and softly pulled it closed behind her.

"Are you sure you want to do this, Tamara?" Faraday asked. "I'm still very alert."

"Please, Matthew," she replied, "I am more than capable of this." She slid her right hand into her pocket and slowly pulled out a derringer. Faraday's blue eyes widened in surprise. "I didn't know you were armed! We've, been riding on that train all this time, and I had no idea."

Tamara looked at him sheepishly. "Actually, Matthew, several nurses were issued guns during the war. I was one." Her eyes grew bleak as she went on, "We were taught how to use them. I thank God I never had to, and I pray that I won't need to tonight." Then she turned to Earl Barlow, who was watching her carefully, and said, "I'm ready, General. Please tell me where to position myself."

Barlow smiled and, extending his elbow, escorted her toward the large courtroom. The general glanced over his shoulder at Faraday, who was still standing at the door to the judges' chambers. The detective nodded sadly and moved quietly into the darkened room.

Four hours later Tamara tiptoed into the dimly lit judges' chambers and gently shook Cole's shoulder. The young agent woke with a start and almost jumped to his feet.

"Cole, it's all right," she hushed him gently. "I didn't mean to startle you. Daniels and his men have not shown up."

Cole rubbed his face groggily and nodded. "Okay, Tamara," he mumbled. "What time is it?"

"It's almost five," she said softly. "Time for you and Buford to take up the watch. The general is waiting for me to tell him you're coming."

"Don't bother going. I'll go at once. You need your sleep. Sit here and rest." He rose, gently took her arm, and guided her to his chair.

"Cole Yeager," she chided him in a whisper. "I often sat up all night long during these past four years...with sick and dying men. These past few hours have been far easier than any of those painful nights." Nevertheless, she sank gratefully into the chair and patted his hand. "Thank you," she murmured and closed her eyes.

Cole smiled down at her and turned to waken Buford Posey. Within a moment the two men slipped silently from the room.

Daniels and his men did not appear during the vigil in the Court House, nor were they seen when the cortege wound its way back to the depot. Faraday and the teams returned to the funeral train oh the evening of May 2, disheartened that the threat from Daniels still existed. For a few moments

Tamara hoped that Daniels had abandoned the scheme. When she said this to Earl Barlow, the general shook his head grimly.

"No," he replied. "He won't. We'll find him in Springfield."

The funeral train finally rolled into Springfield at 7:00 A.M. on Wednesday morning, May 3. Springfield was the smallest of all the cities that held a funeral service. It was so small, in fact, that at the time Lincoln left it four years earlier, he knew every man, woman, and child in the community by name. Upon saying farewell on that cold day in February 1861, he had remarked, "My friends, no one not in my situation can appreciate my feelings of sadness at this parting. To this place, and the kindness of these people, I owe everything. Here I have lived a quarter of a century and have passed from a young to an old man. I now leave, not knowing when, or whether ever, I may return."

He was returning today, and his former friends and neighbors were all on hand to welcome him home.

Because it was so small, Springfield had no hearse to compare with the magnificent funeral coaches of the other cities. The city of St. Louis had offered its own hearse, a beautiful vehicle trimmed in silver and gold and glassed on all four sides. As the coffin was placed inside, two hundred and fifty singers began the first notes of the song that had so stirred the nation during the war that had just ended, "The Battle Hymn of the Republic."

The body was transported to the statehouse, where, again, it would lie for twenty-four hours before making the final journey to the Oak Ridge Cemetery.

After what had seemed to be two weeks of continuous rain, Thursday, May 4, dawned sunny. The temperature rose so quickly that by midday it was blisteringly hot. At sunrise, thirty-six guns were fired in salute, then a single gun was fired at ten-minute intervals throughout the morning until the funeral cortege was ready to begin its two-mile journey to the cemetery.

The Veteran Sergeants carried the coffin from the state-house rotunda and slid it reverently into the hearse. The same choir that had met the train sang, "Children of the Heavenly King, As Ye Journey Sweetly Sing."

Escorted by a military guard of one thousand members, the funeral procession began its final march. In the hot air, heavy with the scent of lilacs, it wound through the streets of Springfield, then traveled down a country road to the cemetery.

Even though thousands marched or rode in the parade, no one spoke. The only sounds were the hollow clomping of the horses' hooves, the rumble of the wheels, the tramp of the soldiers' feet, and the steady, muffled beat of drums that matched the rhythm of a heartbeat—a muted *thump, thump, thump*.

Finally the procession passed under the ever green arch at the cemetery entrance and moved through the little valley between two tree-covered ridges to a receiving vault that had been dug into the hillside. Abraham Lincoln's body would lie in this public tomb until his own, grand sepulcher could be constructed.

Some people protested that ending such an extensive and glorious funeral by putting his body in a public receiving tomb was almost blasphemous. In fact, the city had built a special crypt for the slain President downtown at great expense. But Mary Todd Lincoln, still in Washington, sent word that he was to be buried in the cemetery or she would have the body taken elsewhere. In light of such a threat, the city fathers had no choice but to place Lincoln in the public vault. This pleased others who had argued that it was altogether fitting for a man of the people, the President of a Republic, to spend time with the common man before being transferred to a more ornate chamber that would rival the tombs of kings.

By noon, the ceremony was ended, and the nation's ordeal was over. President Lincoln was placed in the holding tomb beside his young son Willie, whose coffin had been deposited there earlier in the day. The key to the tomb was given to Robert Lincoln, who had arrived by separate train in time for the funeral. The thousands who had thronged to the cemetery hillside started home.

Later that day in downtown Springfield, a crowd stood in front of the governor's mansion listening to a St. Louis band playing not funeral dirges, but happy, energetic tunes. Those songs seemed to lift the somber mood. The two weeks of mourning were officially over, and once again people began to find things to laugh about.

In a hotel room across the street from the governor's mansion, Manley Daniels stood in front of an open window, hoping that a slight breeze would blow into the unbearably hot room to cool him off. Daniels was hiding there with Alan Tatterwall and Lee Hawkins. The music and laughter drifted into the room through the window.

"Listen to them," Daniels sneered sarcastically, his face twisted in a scowl. "Yesterday the whole country was crying. Today they're laughing and carrying on as if nothing ever happened."

"They can only cry for so long," Alan Tatterwall commented.

"Yes, well, we'll give them something else to cry about tonight, eh boys?" Daniels replied, his dark, hooded eyes glittering malevolently. "They won't be so happy when they discover that the decaying corpse they have so tenderly laid to rest is no longer there."

The other two men did not reply for a long moment, then Lee Hawkins sighed. "I guess not," he mumbled.

Daniels, who had been watching the crowd move through the street, turned to look back into the shaded room at Hawkins. "What do you mean, you guess not? Are you having second thoughts?"

"No," Hawkins quickly assured him. "But are you certain it's going to be as easy as you say?"

"Of course I'm certain. We won't even have any digging to do. They didn't bury the body; they just put it in a crypt...all ready for us to take. There'll be nothing to it."

"That's what we thought back in Maryland, but Colonel Yeager nearly caught us. And in Ohio, he had to be the one in that runaway train," Tatterwall reminded him.

"Yes, well, I'm sure his job was to see that Lincoln's body arrived safely in Springfield. He did that...and now he can go home. Nobody will be guarding the cemetery tonight." He scowled derisively again. "What do you think? Do you suppose they plan to post a guard outside his grave from now until eternity?"

"I guess you're right," Hawkins murmured grudgingly.

"You're damned right, I'm right," Daniels growled. "This is going to be the easiest one million dollars anyone ever made. We'll steal the body, demand our ransom, then pick up our money, and leave the country. And all we have to do to get it is take a stroll through the cemetery tonight."

The three plotters were not the only ones waiting for night to fall to put a plan into action. Hidden behind clumps of trees that stood on either side of the President's temporary tomb were Matthew Faraday, Earl Barlow, Buford Posey, Dorsey Evans, and Cole Yeager. By design they had remained in the cemetery after all the other mourners had left. Despite Tamara's protests Faraday had insisted she return to Springfield. It had been a hot, unpleasant afternoon with virtually no breeze to mitigate the unseasonable heat. They all welcomed the onset of evening, even though they knew that once the sun set Daniels and his men were certain to appear.

After sunset heavy clouds began to roll in, blotting out the moon and the stars. The cemetery was not lighted by torches or gas lights, and it was so dark that it was impossible to see for more than a few feet.

"I wonder if we should move closer," Cole whispered to Faraday who was crouching beside him.

"This is as close as we can get and still have some cover," Faraday replied. "Besides, they'll be just as blind as we are. If they're going to be successful in removing the body, they'll have to have a light of some kind. When they arrive, we'll be sure to see them."

The wait seemed interminable. Unable to see anything, Cole felt as though they were inside a dark tunnel. Suddenly a white light blinded him. A thunderstorm was brewing. Every several seconds a jagged streak of lightning flashed across the sky, momentarily revealing the details of the cemetery in a harsh, brilliant glare that hurt his eyes before blackness returned. Seconds after each stark white flash, thunder boomed loudly, roaring like the cannons that had marked the last twenty days.

With each lightning flash the tombstones were eerily highlighted, and long, ghostly shadows were cast over the scene. Cole felt a chill crawl at his neck. Sitting in this cemetery reminded him of the time when he was six or seven and his older brother had dared him to walk through the cemetery that was several hundred yards up the road from his boyhood home. He remembered how loudly his heart had pounded as he stepped through the gate and how he had nearly fainted when a screech owl hooted abruptly, then flew frighteningly close to his head.

Suddenly the wind picked up, rustling and blowing the branches over their heads and making it hard to hear anything else. Drops of rain began pelting them, and the five men automatically hunkered down like turtles retreating into their shells.

Cole wondered if Daniels and his cohorts would show up after all on such a night. Curious to know just how long they had been waiting, he took out his watch and held it up so that during the next lightning flash, he would be able to read the face. But Cole did not learn what time it was.

When the next bolt of lightning streaked across the sky, he saw three men stealthily approaching the tomb. Keeping his eyes riveted on them so he would know where they were when the blackness descended again, he slid his watch back into his pocket. One of them was carrying a lantern, although the light was so carefully shielded that the flame was barely visible.

"There they are," he hissed urgently, nudging Faraday and pointing to the pinpoint of moving light. Evidently Barlow, Buford, and Dorsey had seen them too because Cole heard someone rustling in the clump of trees where they were concealed.

"Daniels!" Barlow shouted. "Give yourself up! Don't try anything!"

Lightning flashed again, illuminating the outlaw trio in its stark glare. The former colonel was peering toward the clump of trees where Barlow and his men were hiding, searching for the source of the voice.

"Damn you!" Daniels called back.

Blackness erased the image. The lantern was quickly extinguished but not before Cole had made a mental note of where it was located. Then there was a flash of gunfire as Daniels fired his pistol at them. Cole heard the bullet whine into the trees that concealed Barlow and his men. The snap and rustle of twigs told him that the men were moving. Cole prayed that they would scurry behind the tombstones.

Cole pulled out his own weapon and shot into the darkness at the flame that had spat from Daniels's gun. But the next bolt of lightning revealed that the threesome had disappeared. The former Union officer had been in hundreds of battles and skirmishes during the four years of the war, and he knew that Daniels and his men—who were also veterans —would take tactical advantage of the storm.

Another gunshot rang out. This time the bullet whistled into the trees above their heads, and Cole and Faraday realized that their position was too vulnerable. They split up, each man going in a different direction and firing as he ran.

The roaring of guns joined the flashing lightning and booming thunder, making the small cemetery seem more like a battlefield than a place of peaceful, eternal repose. Cole felt a sense of unreality, as if the gunfight were something he was dreaming. The harsh flashes of the lightning dimmed his vision, and the ever-moving shadows cast by tree branches would have made it virtually impossible to spot his targets were it not for the orange flames that spat from their pistols.

Daniels and the two men with him knew to fire and move, fire and move—never giving their enemies a stationary target. The three would-be grave robbers kept up a steady barrage of shots, and the lead flew through the night air, whining off the marble gravestones and whistling through the trees.

Then Cole fired at one of the orange flames too quickly for the Rebel to move away, and his bullet found its mark. He heard a gasp, then a cry of pain.

For a moment, they stopped shooting, and the Confederates were silent. Then one of them called, "Colonel Daniels? Colonel, are you all right?"

There was no answer.

Matthew Faraday yelled from his position, "Give it up, men! We've got you covered!"

One of the Rebels called to his accomplice, "Hawkins, what'll we do?"

For answer, the man fired toward Faraday. Then he shouted, "I ain't gonna give up!"

"That's Tatterwall's voice," Barlow called to his men, his voice almost drowned out by the boom of thunder.

Cole fired back in the direction of the shot, and he heard a scream.

"Tatterwall, did he get you?" the third man yelled. "Tatterwall, answer me!"

At first there was no response, then the man groaned, "I'm hit, Hawkins. I'm hit, and Daniels is dead."

"How bad?"

"I don't know."

"Hawkins, Tatterwall, it's me, General Barlow. Give it up," the officer told them insistently.

"What're you doin' over on the Yankee side?" Hawkins cried.

"This isn't the Yankee side anymore," Barlow shouted. "The war's over. The plan I concocted was a bad one—and now, with Daniels dead, so's the idea you men had."

There was silence for a moment, then Hawkins spoke. "General? What's gonna happen to us if we give it up?"

"Nothing," Faraday called. "Come out here and drop your guns, then go on home."

"Just like that?"

"Just like that."

Again there was silence before Hawkins declared, "I don't believe you."

"Believe him, boys," Barlow called back to them. "Dorsey and Buford can tell you it's true." There was a moment's hesitation, then Tatterwall and Hawkins appeared, first as darker shadows in the night and then illuminated by a flash of lightning. Hawkins was holding both hands up, Tatterwall only one, his left arm dangling by his side.

"Come on over here," Faraday called.

The two men did as they were told, crossing over to Cole and Faraday. Reaching them, they dropped their guns. Barlow, Dorsey, and Buford moved to join them.

The storm had abated, and it seemed to Cole that the cessation of the fireworks overhead coincided with the peace achieved below. Some periodic, far-off lightning flashes lit up the scene.

Faraday turned to Barlow and said firmly, "General, I am releasing Alan Tatterwall and Lee Hawkins into your custody. Since you were their commanding officer, I believe you'll know how to handle them. I want you to see that these men take Daniels's body and bury it in that field beyond the cemetery." Then his tone grew gentler, and he went on, "After you're finished, I want you and your compatriots to go home."

"That's it?" Tatterwall cried in disbelief. "You're really gonna let us go, just like that?"

Nodding slowly, Faraday echoed, "Just like that." He gazed at Barlow, Dorsey, and Buford. "The only thing I ask is that you tell no one what happened here tonight. The world must never learn of the attempt to steal Abraham Lincoln's body."

"You have my word on it, sir," Barlow assured him. He looked at Buford and Dorsey.

"Mine, too," Dorsey agreed, and Buford nodded his head vigorously.

Dorsey glared at Tatterwall, and Buford rested a heavy, convincing hand on Hawkins's shoulder. Both men mumbled their agreement grudgingly.

Barlow nodded knowingly and reached out to shake first Faraday's hand, then Cole's. He grinned at the young agent.

"Miss Goodnight is a lucky woman," he said warmly. "She's getting one hell of a man."

"How did you—?" Cole began, then he, too, laughed. "Never mind. It obviously wasn't much of a secret." Then his expression grew sober, and he looked thoughtfully at the general. "Perhaps someday, after all the bitterness the war has caused has been forgotten, we will meet again—as friends."

Barlow returned Cole's intent gaze for a long moment. "Perhaps," he finally said softly. Then, turning to his men, he declared, "Let's get going. We have a job to do, and it's a long way home." Suddenly another bolt of lightning cast its unearthly glare in a much brighter flash than the ones of a moment earlier. Something stark and gaunt loomed beside Lincoln's tomb. It looked like a very tall man wearing a top hat. Barlow gasped. Then a second lightning flash revealed that it was merely the stump of a tree.

Laughing uneasily, the general murmured, "For a moment I thought he was still with us."

"He is," Faraday said gently. "And I have a feeling he always will be."

A LOOK AT THE TOWN MARSHAL

BY ROBERT VAUGHAN

THE TOWN MARSHAL is ripped from the annals of authentic American history of the Old West. Its two main participants, James Cooper and Henry Newton Brown, form a close friendship when, along with Billy the Kid, they fight in the Lincoln County War. After that, James and Henry move on, their bond of friendship growing even stronger as James becomes a crusading newspaper editor and Henry, a town marshal feared by outlaws and lauded by his peers and the towns he served.

But something goes wrong, and in an emotive moment, the two best friends find themselves face to face in a dramatic and poignant confrontation.

AVAILABLE NOW

ABOUT THE AUTHOR

Robert Vaughan sold his first book when he was 19. That was 57 years and nearly 500 books ago. He wrote the novelization for the miniseries *Andersonville*. Vaughan wrote, produced, and appeared in the History Channel documentary *Vietnam Homecoming*. His books have hit the NYT bestseller list seven times. He has won the Spur Award, the PORGIE Award (Best Paperback Original), the Western Fictioneers Lifetime Achievement Award, received the Readwest President's Award for Excellence in Western Fiction, is a member of the American Writers Hall of Fame and is a Pulitzer Prize nominee. Vaughn is also a retired army officer, helicopter pilot with three tours in Vietnam. And received the Distinguished Flying Cross, the Purple Heart, The Bronze Star with three oak leaf clusters, the Air Medal for valor with 35 oak leaf clusters, the Army Commendation Medal, the Meritorious Service Medal, and the Vietnamese Cross of Gallantry.

Find more great titles by Robert Vaughan at Wolfpack Publishing.

Made in the USA
Lexington, KY
25 April 2019